"I'm not nervous," she denied too quickly and too vehemently

"I'm just worried what everyone will think of you sleeping in the main house."

"What would they think, Bree?" he asked, in a way that suggested all kinds of sinful things. Then his tone took on a bitter, hard edge. "After all, we're family, you having married my brother and all."

The censure in his gaze hurt more than she thought possible. Her reason for marrying Boyd had been desperation. But Tyler would always assume the worst.

"Fine," she said tightly, and left. "Just relax, Brianne," she coached herself. Her troubling thoughts were further complicated by the sleeping boy in the room across the hall. Tyler's son. Guilt pricked her conscience. She deliberately pushed it aside. What good would come if she revealed the truth of Daniel's parentage now? Tyler was hardly a stable role model for her son. He'd already proved with a nine-year absence that he'd run at the first sign of trouble.

One man had already destroyed her son's trust. She vowed she wouldn't give Tyler the opportunity to do the same.

Janelle Denison has read romances ever since she was in high school. She never intended to become a writer, but her love of books and romance led to writing the kind of emotionally satisfying stories she's enjoyed from Harlequin over the years. While perfecting her craft, she worked as a construction secretary, but recently decided to quit her "day job" to write full-time.

Janelle lives in Southern California with her engineer husband, whose support and encouragement have enabled her to follow her dream of writing, and two young daughters, who keep life interesting and give her plenty of ideas for the young characters she includes in her books.

Janelle Denison also writes for Harlequin® Temptation®.

Look out later in 1999 for Janelle Denison's next Harlequin Romance® novel, *Bride Included*, another great book in our ongoing BACK TO THE RANCH series:
Eleven years ago, Seth O'Connor had left Josie McAllister brokenhearted—and pregnant! Josie was convinced that the sexy bachelor had found it easier to believe the lies about her reputation than accept the truth—that he was the father of her child! But now Seth was back—and in his hands was a legal document that laid claim not only to the McAllister ranch but to Josie, too!

Books by Janelle Denison

HARLEQUIN ROMANCE
3531—READY-MADE BRIDE

HARLEQUIN TEMPTATION
679—PRIVATE PLEASURES
682—PRIVATE FANTASIES

A Dad for Daniel
Janelle Denison

TORONTO • NEW YORK • LONDON
AMSTERDAM • PARIS • SYDNEY • HAMBURG
STOCKHOLM • ATHENS • TOKYO • MILAN • MADRID
PRAGUE • WARSAW • BUDAPEST • AUCKLAND

To my beautiful daughters, Danielle and Kellie,
for making my life so rich and rewarding,
not to mention challenging. I love you both.
To my editor, Gillian Green:
thank you for giving my stories a home.
And as always, to Don: a wonderful husband,
a great dad and the best friend I've ever had.

ISBN 0-373-03546-2

A DAD FOR DANIEL

First North American Publication 1999.

Copyright © 1998 by Janelle R. Denison.

Printed in U.S.A.

PROLOGUE

TYLER WHITMORE knew the malicious gleam in his half-brother's eyes meant trouble. It always did. Boyd had hated him from the moment he'd been born, and there hadn't been a day that went by that he hadn't expressed that hatred.

With a sense of unease twisting through him, Tyler stepped more fully into the ranch office. Ignoring Boyd's smug expression, Tyler faced the man who'd raised him, loving him unconditionally, even though he'd been another man's child. Landon—Boyd's father. "You wanted to talk to me?"

Determination filled Landon's pale blue eyes. "I'm sorry, Tyler," he said, his tone grim. "But I'm shutting down the reining operation."

Shock momentarily rendered Tyler speechless. He'd spent three years raising, training and selling reining horses on Whitmore Acres. It had been a new venture for the ranch outside of breeding quarter horses and the cutting operation that Boyd managed, but Tyler couldn't fathom any reason to cease such a profitable enterprise.

Tyler shook his head, frowning. "I don't understand..."

Landon sighed, suddenly looking as old and worn as his sixty-four years. "Boyd tells me the reining operation is losing money."

"What?" His tight, incredulous tone boomed in the small office. "How can I be losing money when I've made a substantial profit from each of the mares I've sold?"

"Your expenses exceed your profit." Landon gestured toward the accounting journal spread open on his desk. "The books show a loss. The cutting operation can't afford to carry both ventures any longer."

Jaw clenched hard against the simmering anger, Tyler glanced pointedly at his half-brother leaning insolently against a tall filing cabinet across the room. When Landon had retired two years earlier, he'd appointed Boyd in charge of the ranch's finances. Knowing Boyd's weakness for drinking, gambling, and womanizing, Tyler suspected Boyd was skimming from the reining profits to support his excessive spending habits. Yet he had no proof, and Boyd was cunning enough to cover any trail of paperwork that would point a guilty finger his way.

But Tyler had no compunction voicing his own suspicions. "Maybe you ought to keep an eye on the person managing the finances."

"Are you insinuating something, little *brother?*" Boyd asked, his bland tone giving nothing away.

Tyler's gaze narrowed. "Yeah, that you've been stealing, for starters—from my reining operation to cover your own losses."

Boyd had the audacity to look affronted. "That's a mighty big accusation, and a defamation of my good character."

Tyler snorted at that, knowing beneath the good-ol'-boy facade he put on for Landon's sake hid a mean and spiteful person. "You just won't be satisfied until I'm completely miserable, will you? Until you've taken away everything that ever mattered to me." It had always been that way, Boyd destroying or stealing whatever he'd coveted—and took pleasure in doing so. Why should this have been any different? Because he thought he'd had Landon's support. That Landon didn't believe in him hurt more than he thought possible.

"I think you're taking this a little too personally, Tyler." Boyd's tone was reasonable, which Tyler knew was all for Landon's benefit. "I can't help it if your reining operation is a big flop. We can't have it sucking the ranch dry, now can we?"

Twenty-three years of his half-brother's emotional cruelty came to a boiling head, filling Tyler with an impotent rage he couldn't control. Crossing the room in less than two heartbeats, he grabbed Boyd by the front of his shirt and slammed him against the wall. Boyd didn't struggle to defend himself. No, the look in his eyes dared Tyler to hit him, which infuriated Tyler even more. Boyd always acted exemplary around Landon. Only Tyler witnessed and experienced the intensity of Boyd's hatred, and just how vindictive he could be. It would never change.

Tyler tightened his fists against Boyd's chest. "You son of a bitch," he said in low growl of fury. "You know damn well that the reining operation is holding it's own!"

"Break it up, boys!" Landon rounded his desk and pushed Tyler away from Boyd, his expression thunderous. "I won't tolerate this kind of behavior, Tyler."

"The reining operation is *mine*," Tyler said fiercely. He'd worked hard to establish himself, and despite Boyd's claim, he knew the venture was successful. "I'm not letting it go."

Landon's face turned an angry shade of red. "I'm not giving you a choice, Tyler. I'm cutting the reining operation loose and that's final!" With those words ringing in the air, Landon turned on his booted heel and left the office.

Boyd stepped toward the door and brushed carelessly

at the wrinkles Tyler had put in his shirt. "I guess it pays to be the boss's *real* son, doesn't it? You're nothing but a bastard, Tyler, a charity case our mother saddled Landon with when she left him. This precious ranch you covet will never be yours, because you don't have an ounce of Whitmore blood running through your veins. Landon's decision today proves that." He stopped before leaving the office, a triumphant smile curling his mouth. "I wonder how your sweet, innocent Brianne is going to feel about you losing the reining operation, and that she'll never have the ranch she loves so much."

Tyler went stone cold inside. Brianne loved *him*, not Whitmore Acres, he wanted to yell, but his chest had tightened to the point that it hurt to breathe, and his half-brother had beat a hasty exit. As Boyd's words sank past his rage, he realized that Boyd was right. Without the reining operation he had nothing to offer Brianne Taylor, the girl he'd meant to marry, and had sworn to take away from her drunken father's neglect.

Tyler wanted to roar at the injustice of Boyd's cruelty, but what had transpired today with Landon was proof that he didn't belong on Whitmore Acres. Within the hour he'd packed his meager belongings and left the ranch, determined to find work elsewhere as a reining trainer and prove Landon, and Boyd, wrong.

It had taken him six weeks for his temper to cool enough for him to consider going home to mend the rift between him and Landon, and return for Brianne. Despite his brother's claim, he couldn't believe the girl he loved was shallow enough to want him only for the security Whitmore Acres offered.

He'd been wrong.

He'd arrived back in town on the very morning Brianne was to marry Boyd. That bit of unsettling news had been imparted by Gus, the old man who owned and attended the small town's gas station where Tyler had pulled in to gas up and mentally prepare himself for the confrontation that lay ahead.

Unwilling to believe that Brianne would be so faithless, he'd immediately headed toward the courthouse. He'd pulled up to a corner stoplight just in time to see a small crowd gathering outside, then Boyd and Brianne descend the stairs hand in hand. In her plain white dress and the crown of flowers haloing her blond head, Brianne looked pale and fragile, but all Tyler saw was the scheming woman she'd become, settling for whatever Whitmore could offer her a better life. And with him off Whitmore Acres, Boyd stood to gain everything.

Her betrayal cut as sharp as a knife straight to his heart.

Then he'd caught sight of Landon standing off to the side, smiling as he watched the newly-wedded pair, and something within Tyler died at that moment. In its place grew a black rage and bitterness. He was the bastard son, and he didn't belong. Never would. After losing the reining operation, Landon's respect, and now Brianne, there was nothing left for him to come home for.

Instead of making the left-hand turn that would put him and his truck in full view of the wedding party, he drove straight past...right back out of town. And he'd never looked back.

CHAPTER ONE

AFTER nine years of drifting, the past had finally caught up to Tyler Whitmore in a small town in Oregon where he'd spent the last six months working as a trainer on the Circle E.

Warily, Tyler eyed the man who'd introduced himself as a P.I. representing the law firm of Wilkins and Moore—more specifically, he'd been retained by Jed Wilkins, the man who'd been Landon's personal attorney since Tyler was a boy.

"I've been trying to find you for the past seven years," the man said, his smile as amicable as his personality. "But you've been a difficult man to track. You don't stay in one place long, and you're not in a habit of leaving a forwarding address. Finally, I got a solid lead before you could take off again."

Tyler found all that information interesting, but not as intriguing as what the man's purpose for locating him could be. "Now that you've found me, what can I do for you?"

"I'm here to deliver a letter from Jed Wilkins, Landon Whitmore's attorney." He reached inside his jacket pocket and pulled out an envelope and handed it Tyler's way. "Why don't you read the correspondence, and then I'll be happy to answer any questions you might have."

Tyler hesitated, his gaze sliding to the letter—a direct link to a past he'd tried so hard to put behind him. Finally, he reached out and took it before he changed his mind. Turning away, he tore open the flap and unfolded the stationery, wondering if Landon had finally decided to formally disown him after all these years.

The correspondence began with, *I regret to inform you...* and even though Tyler *knew* what would follow that statement, he forced himself to keep reading. According to the letter, Landon had died seven years ago, and his Last Will and Testament named Tyler Scott Whitmore equal heir of Whitmore Acres.

Tyler's head reeled, and he lost his breath for a second, the sensation like that of being tossed by a wild bronc. Shock gave way to deeper feelings of grief and guilt, but before he could fully surrender to either surfacing emotion, he struggled to finish the correspondence, only to receive another devastating blow. His half-brother, Boyd, had died three years ago, and his portion of the Whitmore Estate had reverted to his widow, Brianne Taylor Whitmore.

He closed his eyes and let out a slow, deep breath. He owned half of Whitmore Acres. The thought blew his mind. And Brianne, the girl he'd fallen hopelessly in love with, the girl who'd betrayed him in the cruelest way possible, owned the other portion by default of Boyd's death.

How damned ironic, Tyler thought, unable to stop the bitterness still left lingering from her long-ago deception.

In a startling, painful moment Tyler realized the only two people who'd once been his family no longer existed. Hell, he didn't even know who his mother was; she'd abandoned all of them when he'd been an infant. His real father could have been any one of the ranch hands she'd slept with during her marriage to Landon. He had no one. And for all the years he'd spent drifting from one ranch to another training horses, he had nothing but a truck, trailer, and his horse, Sweet Justice, to call his own.

Stuffing the letter back into the envelope, Tyler turned and faced the P.I. again. "What happens now?"

"My job is finished." The younger man grinned, obviously glad of that. "I'll let Jed Wilkins know I've found you, but it'll be up to you to get in touch with him to claim your inheritance. From there, all other parties involved will be notified."

Once the P.I. left, Tyler reread the letter, missing the man who'd been the only father figure he'd ever known. Despite what had happened in the past, Landon had left him half of Whitmore Acres. Despite that he wasn't Landon's true son, despite Boyd's lies, and despite how selfish he'd been in shunning the only father he'd ever known and not being there for him in the last days of his life. Still, Landon had forgiven him.

Scrubbing a hand over his tense jaw, Tyler mulled those thoughts over in his mind. Eventually, he came to terms with the stunning, unexpected news of his inheritance and Landon's death, though he was certain the grief and sorrow would take more time to ease.

Instead of dwelling on things he couldn't change, Tyler looked toward the future. Landon had left him a legacy for a reason, and Tyler intended to embrace his generous gift and make it prosper...to use it to rebuild the dreams that had been shattered so long ago and possibly lay to rest the demons of the past.

It was time to go home, to Whitmore Acres.

Tap, tap, tap.

Brianne Whitmore bolted upright in bed, her heart thudding in her chest as she strained to hear the noise that had awakened her. She hadn't always been a light sleeper, but the years she'd been married to Boyd had taught her to never let her guard down, and that included when she slept. After he'd died, her body was so used to waking at the slightest sound that the protective instinct was now deeply ingrained.

She glanced at the digital clock on her nightstand, which glowed 11:26 p.m. It was a warm summer night, and although her window was open, there wasn't the slightest breeze to rustle the leaves in the tree outside her bedroom, or cause a branch to scrape along the side of the house.

She'd begun to think she'd imagined the sound when it came again and she was able to identify it—a light knocking on the front door. The tapping was followed by a low, masculine voice tentatively calling, "Brianne?"

Her first thought was that it was her foreman, Jasper, and there had been some kind of emergency on the ranch. Spurred into action by that possibility, she tossed off the covers and hurried down the landing of stairs and into the foyer. She switched on the porch light, flipped the locks and opened the door.

"Is everything okay—" The breathless words died on her lips. It wasn't Jasper, that much was evident by the wide, muscular chest covered in blue chambray that she was staring at, instead of into the hazel eyes and old, weathered face of Whitmore Acres' longtime foreman.

No, this man was tall, lean, and way too imposing. She tilted her head back to see his face, which was shadowed by the brim of a chocolate-colored Stetson pulled low over his forehead. The only thing she could see was the dark stubble lining a strong jaw, and full lips pressed into a grim line.

From what she saw, there was nothing soft, welcoming, or familiar about this man. Yet he'd known her name. A frisson of unease slithered down her spine. Realizing the foolishness of opening her door to a stranger—in her nightgown, and the middle of the night, no less!—she retreated a step and attempted to slam the door shut.

A large hand shot out inches from her goal, and a panicked sound caught in her throat. Adrenaline rushed through her veins, and she pressed her full weight, slight as it was, against the door, her one and only thought to protect her and her son.

"Brianne, it's me," a gruff voice announced. "Open the goddamned door!"

It's me. Brianne froze, but didn't do as he demanded. Instead, she slowly and carefully peeked through the crack between the door and threshold, as wide as the boot he'd managed to wedge there.

He jammed his hat back and she caught his ominous frown before her gaze met strikingly dark blue eyes. Eyes that once had the ability to turn her inside out with wanting, eyes that had haunted her dreams for too long. Her breath left her as recognition hit with the force of a head-on collision.

Her body went slack from shock. She let the door ease back open as she stared at the man who'd broken her heart nine years earlier. Joy, anger, hurt and fear, *especially fear,* all warred within her. Why had he shown up now? she thought frantically, after all the years of no word from him. And just when she'd finally made a stable life for herself and her son. *He* had the power to destroy all her hard-earned dreams.

Her hand fluttered nervously to the bodice of her thin cotton nightgown. *"Tyler."* His name escaped on a croak.

A smile curved his mouth, more contemptuous than hospitable. "Hello, *Mrs. Whitmore.*"

Somehow, Tyler knew she'd married his brother. Dear Lord, had he discovered *why?* Did he know his brother and Landon were dead? Did he know he now owned half of Whitmore Acres? She had no idea why he'd come home, and she dreaded the answers as much as she anticipated them.

She'd always known the possibility of Tyler returning existed—it had been Landon's wish he be located and Jed Wilkins had done his best to track Tyler. But after all the false leads and the years that had passed without any contact with him, she'd begun to believe he'd found something better than Whitmore Acres.

Obviously, not so.

Pushing her panic aside, she forced anger to take over. "Dammit, Tyler, you scared the hell out of me!"

His unapologetic gaze flickered over her, and her heart leaped beneath her breast. Not from fear this time, but in a purely female response to the man Tyler had become, all lean strength and blatant male sensuality.

Once he'd finished his lazy perusal, he lifted a dark brow that matched the sable hair curling over the collar of his shirt. "Now, is that any way to greet an old...friend?"

Her face warmed at the subtle reference to their past relationship. They'd been more than friends, which made her response to him so disturbing. She'd thought she was over Tyler Whitmore, and she hated that he still had the ability to stir her emotions, despite the heartache she'd suffered because of him.

"It's the way I'll treat anyone who's prowling around the property in the middle of night," she replied in a business-like manner.

"You'll have to pardon my bad manners," he said in a droll tone as he turned and lifted a black duffel bag from the porch swing. "In the shuffle of the last nine years I seemed to have lost my house key."

Taking advantage of the distance he'd put between them, and not ready for him to invade her home, she stepped out of the house and onto the porch. She crossed her arms over her chest and drew a steady breath that did little to soothe the tension within her. "You could have at least called to let me know to expect you."

"And spoil the surprise? Nah, this was too much fun. It's been quite a homecoming."

Annoyance rippled through her. "If you think you can just come back after all this time and pick up where you left off, think again, Tyler." Old, buried emotions welled in her, banding her chest. She glanced away, not wanting Tyler to see the pain she knew reflected in her eyes.

"I have no intention of picking up where we left off," he said softly. "Too much has changed."

He was right. Everything *had* changed. Her. Him. The ranch. A fact of life, but it still filled her with sadness.

They stood out on the dim porch, staring warily at each other like the adversaries they'd become. The silence grew as thick as molasses. Good manners dictated she invite him in, but she couldn't bring herself to issue the invitation. She had so much at stake beyond that threshold, and she wasn't sure she was emotionally equipped for him to discover the many secrets that lay beyond.

Finally, Tyler shifted on his feet and sighed wearily. "Are you going to ask me in, or are we going to stand here all night staring at one another?"

"It's nearly midnight!" She was being irrational, she knew, but couldn't help herself.

"Yes, it is," he replied calmly. "I've been on the road for hours and I'm tired. I'd like to get some sleep."

She glanced beyond his shoulder toward the barn, then opened her mouth to make a not-so-gracious suggestion.

"I'm not sleeping in the stables, so don't bother suggesting it," he cut her off impatiently. "I don't know what you're so nervous about."

"I'm not nervous!" she denied too quickly and too vehemently. In an effort to force herself to relax, she brushed back the stray strands of blond hair that had escaped her braid. Feeling slightly more in control of her emotions, she reached for a plausible excuse. "I'm just worried what everyone will think of you sleeping in the main house."

"What would they think, Bree?" he asked in a way that suggested all kinds of sinful things. Then his tone took on a bitter, hard edge. "After all, we're family, you having married my brother and all."

The censure in his gaze hurt more than she thought possible. If only Tyler knew Boyd had married her out of vengeance, an attempt to destroy his half-brother by claiming what had been Tyler's. Her reasons for marrying Boyd had been more desperate. But Tyler would always assume the worst. To reveal the truth now would threaten what she treasured above all else.

She forced a smile. "Fine," she said tightly, and stepped back to push the door open for him.

He brushed past her, bulging duffel bag in hand, and she followed him into the house, advancing no further than the entryway. She snapped on the tall, antique brass lamp by the door. Muted light spilled into the adjoining living room, and Tyler stepped through the double-width doorway.

"I'm going upstairs for a minute." She wanted to put on her robe, and needed a few moments alone to collect her rattled composure. "Go ahead and make yourself comfortable."

He briefly glanced her way. "Don't worry about me. I'll be fine."

In her bedroom, Brianne grabbed her pink cotton robe. Slipping it over her nightgown, she belted the sash then began pacing the floor next to her bed. Maybe if she stayed in her room long enough he'd leave. Better yet, she wanted to crawl back into the safe haven of her bed, surrender to a deep sleep, and wake in the morning with this whole ordeal being nothing more than an awful nightmare.

"Just relax, Brianne," she coached herself. Drawing a calming breath, she released it slowly.

Though some of the stress ebbed from her body, she could only think how much she had at stake: the ranch she'd revived from near bankruptcy. The house and home she'd lovingly created for her and her son. And now, the tangle of emotions she'd buried after Tyler had deserted her that were struggling to resurface. Her troubling thoughts were further complicated by the sleeping boy in the room across the hall. Tyler's son.

Needing to reassure herself Daniel was tucked safely in bed, she slipped into his room. The sign posted on the door, Enter At Your Own Risk, meant exactly what it stated. Maneuvering her way to Daniel's bed in the dark was like walking through a minefield of sports gear, clothing, and toys.

Daniel stirred in his bed, the sheets rustling with the movement. "Mom?" he murmured sleepily.

"Shh, honey," she said soothingly, brushing a lock of blond hair off his brow.

He murmured something unintelligible, then rolled onto his back, sprawling his lanky body on the twin-size bed that in another couple of years would undoubtedly be too short for him.

Crossing her arms over her middle, she stared at her sleeping son, her throat constricting with emotion. Except for his blue eyes, Daniel possessed her fair coloring and features. There was no reason why Tyler wouldn't believe Daniel was Boyd's son.

Guilt pricked her conscience. She deliberately pushed

it aside. What good would come if she revealed the truth of Daniel's parentage now? Tyler was hardly a stable role model for her son. Regardless of Tyler's inheritance, she couldn't trust him to stick around for any length of time. He'd already proved with a nine-year absence that he'd run at the first sign of trouble.

One man had already destroyed her son's trust. She vowed she wouldn't give Tyler the opportunity to do the same.

She'd changed the interior of the house. Drastically.

Tyler didn't recognize the living room as the male sanctuary it had been in his youth, with sturdy, mismatched furniture and bits of masculine paraphernalia strewn from one end of the room to another.

He took off his Stetson, and with a flick of his wrist he sent it sailing to the far end of the sofa next to his duffel bag. Stepping around the mauve-upholstered recliner with the floral arm sleeves, he moved to the fireplace. He digested all the changes, feeling like a stranger in what used to be his home. Absently touching a fragile crystal rose on the mantel, he breathed deeply. Instead of drawing in the familiar scent of tobacco and leather, he inhaled a lighter fragrance of flowers and something infinitely soft and feminine. Like Brianne.

Ignoring the current of warmth settling in his belly, Tyler shoved away from the hearth and prowled the room restlessly. Despite Brianne's attempt to add a woman's touch to the house, Tyler could still feel Landon's presence. He could still picture how he and Landon had watched "Gunsmoke" every Sunday night with a huge bowl of popcorn, or sat on the floor cleaning their shotguns late at night after a day of hunting.

But those days were gone forever, never to be recaptured.

He squeezed his eyes closed for a brief moment, the news of Landon's death still staggering him. The guilt and regret of the past tore at him. And he had no one to blame for his deep, emotional torment but himself.

The sound of footsteps padding down the stairs brought Tyler out of his thoughts. He glanced toward the doorway to the foyer just as Brianne rounded the corner.

For modesty's sake, he assumed, she'd donned an ankle length cotton robe, but the haphazard way she'd tied the sash only served to accentuate her full breasts and the alluring dip and swell of waist and hips. The front opened as she walked, tantalizing him with glimpses of long, graceful legs.

He lifted his gaze to her face. She'd been pretty at eighteen. At twenty-seven she was achingly beautiful. Her face had matured, each feature more prominent and defined. Her complexion was smooth, like porcelain, which set off her wide amber eyes. She'd secured her long blond hair into a braid, but that didn't stop him from remembering the soft, silky texture of those strands sliding through his fingers.

She continued into the living room and stopped by the mauve recliner. Reluctantly, she met his gaze. "Tyler, there's something I need to tell you."

He was more than a little curious what that might be. "Yes?"

"I don't know if you're aware of this or not..." She took a deep breath, then said on a rush of expelled air, "but Landon and Boyd are dead."

He rubbed the suddenly tense muscles at the base of his neck. "Yeah, I know," he said regretfully.

Her fingers worried the tip of the braid resting just above the swell of her breast. "Is that why you came back?"

The question was asked hesitantly, but Tyler caught the prying note to her voice. "Among other reasons." He kept his words deliberately vague.

Her mouth pursed in irritation, and he nearly smiled. He was beginning to understand the quiet tension surrounding her. Judging by her startling reaction to seeing him tonight, he guessed she didn't know that Landon's attorney had finally located him, and that he knew of his inheritance. He wondered if she planned to tell him, or if she'd just bide her time and hope he left without inquiring. She'd married Boyd for the ranch and been sole manager of Whitmore Acres for the past three years. Why would she want a partner now?

Deciding to let her wonder about his intentions, he walked toward her. He stopped so close the tips of his boots touched her bare toes. She tilted her head back, meeting his gaze with a fiery defiance that stirred his blood. She had every opportunity to move away, but didn't budge.

"What other reasons?" she asked boldly, a slight tremor in her voice, as if she was just as affected by his nearness as he was by hers.

He was impressed, and annoyed by her tenacity. Lifting his hand, he gently touched her cheek, intentionally shaking up that unflappable pride straightening her spine. Her breath caught and her eyes widened, granting him a measure of satisfaction.

"I guess I just got a hankerin' for a home-cooked meal," he drawled. "But I suppose that can wait until tomorrow."

She slapped his hand away and glared. "You can starve for all I care." She moved away, and when she'd put enough distance between them she turned back around, looking prim and all business-like again. "About Landon and Boyd—"

"It's late, Brianne," he said, too mentally and emotionally exhausted to discuss the details of Landon's and Boyd's deaths. "How about we talk about everything in the morning?"

"Fine." Her own relief at postponing the inevitable was nearly palpable. "Let me get you a pillow and blanket so you can sleep on the couch." She started out of the living room to retrieve the items.

"There are four bedrooms in this house," he said, stopping her before she could escape. "Surely there's an extra one I can use."

She glanced back at him, pausing long enough for him to realize she had no intention of issuing an invitation beyond him sleeping on the couch. She was treating him like a one-night guest. An *unwelcome* guest.

He nodded toward the adjoining hallway leading to a bathroom and extra room. "What about the bedroom downstairs?"

She pushed her fists into the side pockets in her robe. "That's my sewing room now."

"And the rooms upstairs?"

Again, the slightest hesitation. "The master bedroom is mine, and your old bedroom now belongs to my son."

My son. Her and Boyd's son.

Her softly spoken admission hit Tyler harder than he would have expected, and he smothered his unexpected envy with a dose of sarcasm. "Things sure do have a way of changing, now don't they?"

"What did you expect, Tyler?" she shot back. "You've been gone *nine* years!"

Despite the angry thrust of her chin, he could have sworn there were tears in her eyes. Damn, why had he provoked her like that? The answer came too easily, and he wasn't all that proud of his reasons, either. He'd wanted to hurt her the way she'd hurt him so long ago.

Because of their tangled past, things between them were bound to be strained. Seeing her again made old bitter emotions rise to the surface. But Tyler also realized he needed to maintain some civility to gain her cooperation. He had big plans for his half of the ranch.

With that personal oath in mind, he pushed old betrayals aside and softened his tone. "That leaves one more room. Or is that occupied by another child?"

"No, it's a guest room."

"Perfect." He grabbed his duffel bag and Stetson, ready to follow her to the vacant room.

She didn't move. "There's only a daybed with a twin-size mattress smaller than the width of your shoulders."

A slight exaggeration, he was sure. "I'll take my chances. It's got to be more comfortable than the couch." He stopped in front of her and let a slow smile spread across his lips. "Unless you'd like to offer your bed? I'll just bet you have a big, comfy mattress that would sleep two just fine."

Her face flushed, and he watched the pulse at the base of her throat flutter. Her cool gaze, however, gave away nothing. "The guest bedroom is all yours." She smiled sweetly—too sweetly, he thought—then started for the stairs. "Don't say that I didn't try and warn you."

He followed her up to the second landing, more than satisfied that he'd at least won this small battle of wills. He had bigger challenges to conquer, but this was enough of a start to let her know he could be just as determined and headstrong as she.

They passed the master bedroom, and as he casually peered inside the open doorway, he saw that a feminine haven had replaced what had once been Landon's masculine domain. The door was closed to the next room, which had been his as a boy. The Enter At Your Own Risk sign posted made him smile. Finally, they reached the room Boyd had occupied as a youth—now the guest room.

Brianne pushed the door open and switched on the wall light, letting him precede her into the room. "Here you go."

The smugness in her voice should have warned him, but there was nothing that could have prepared him for what he encountered—a room transformed by floral patterns, frilly throw pillows and curtains, and more ruffles and lace than a cowboy knew what to do with. His gaze lit on the daybed she'd mentioned, and he nearly groaned.

She hadn't exaggerated on the size. The twin-size frame was constructed of a swirled design he suspected was built more for a woman than the durability to support a grown man. And the mattress was a tad bit small—about five inches too short and at least that much too narrow for his frame.

He turned to her and flashed a smile. "Like I said, 'perfect.'"

She actually smirked! "Try and have a good night's sleep."

"Oh, I'm sure I will. You know what they say, there's nothing like Home Sweet Home." He dropped his bag on the bed and unzipped it, rummaging through the contents for the old gray cotton sweatpants he slept in. "By the way, I parked my truck and trailer down by the barn. And I put my mare, Sweet Justice, in the holding corral next to the barn. Will that be okay?"

Brianne shifted closer to the open door. Now she knew why she hadn't heard Tyler's truck pull in. The facilities were sectioned from the main house by a large circular drive and a hundred yards of rolling green lawn. "Your horse should be fine for the night."

He nodded, and Brianne took that as her cue to leave

so he could change and get a few hours' rest. She'd almost made it out of the room but a nagging question stopped her. She glanced over her shoulder.

He was unbuckling his belt, obviously not caring if she watched him undress. The leather hissed in the quiet room as he slid the strap from his jeans.

She swallowed to ease the sudden dryness in her throat, but nothing could stop the racing of her heart. "Tyler?"

His hand stilled on the button of his jeans. He lifted his gaze and met hers, his eyes glowing darkly. He arched a brow. "Yes?"

"How long do you plan on staying?" Her voice was soft, a hushed whisper filled with anticipation.

The slight curving of his mouth could have been a smile. "Indefinitely."

That's what she'd been afraid of.

CHAPTER TWO

WHEN life dealt Brianne disaster, she baked. By seven that same morning the rich fragrance of chocolate permeated the first floor of the house. The kitchen resembled a bakery, with dirty bowls and baking ingredients strewn across the tiled countertop.

Brianne didn't create German chocolate cakes and thick, double fudge brownies so *she* could wallow in the calorie-laden desserts. She baked for the sole purpose of relaxing.

This morning, however, her brand of therapy lacked its normal calming effect. The thought of the unavoidable discussion with Tyler had her on edge. If Tyler didn't know about his inheritance, it was up to her to tell him.

She wasn't looking forward to the task, or a possible confrontation, though she knew one or both was inevitable. Most of all, she wasn't prepared to lose half of everything she'd worked so hard to attain to a man who might be frivolous enough to sell his portion of the estate, just so he could continue with his drifting existence.

Grabbing a quilted mitt, she pulled a tin of muffins from the oven. She touched the browned top of her banana nut muffins to determine whether or not they were done, giving the chore her complete attention to avoid the thoughts tumbling through her mind.

"Do you always bake so enthusiastically first thing in the morning or are you planning a Sunday afternoon bake sale?"

Brianne started at the deep, slumberous timbre of

Tyler's voice, the sound warm and intimate and very destructive to her nervous system. The tin slipped from her grasp and clattered to the counter. She shot an annoyed look over her shoulder, and wished she hadn't.

Tyler stood in the doorway, his shoulder propped against the casing. He looked rumpled and entirely too sexy for having had only a few hours' sleep. The lazy half-smile on his face hiked the temperature in the room by another ten degrees.

His broad chest was bare, and more defined and muscular than she remembered. A light sprinkling of hair swirled around flat brown nipples and arrowed down his lean torso. The mesmerizing trail disappeared into the waistband of his sweats.

Realizing she was staring, she jerked her gaze from him, trying to ignore the flush of awareness spreading across her skin. She passed the back of her hand across her damp brow, suddenly self-conscious of how dowdy she must look in an oversize shirt, pink leggings and smudges of flour for makeup. Angry at herself for caring, she concentrated on righting the muffins that had rolled across the counter.

Tyler strolled into the kitchen, eyeing the muffins, a chocolate cake yet to be frosted, and a pan of raspberry shortbread squares on the counter. "So, what's with the baking frenzy?"

"I couldn't sleep." Which was the truth. After spending hours tossing and turning, she'd given up trying to get some rest.

"Sorry 'bout that," he said, not sounding sorry at all. Stopping beside her, he reached for a muffin.

She sidestepped away and turned off the oven, knowing she could bake for the next week and not find the solace she craved. "Did you sleep okay?" Why did she care, considering she would have preferred he slept in the barn, or in his truck.

"As well as to be expected, considering that sorry excuse for a bed I slept on."

She dropped a measuring cup into the soapy water in the sink. "Sorry." This time, *her* voice held no remorse.

He shrugged and took a bite of his muffin. A moment later he lifted a brow in mild surprise. "Not bad."

She wasn't sure if that was a compliment or not, but took it as one. He scratched his chest as he finished the muffin, and she wanted to scream as the raspy, sexy sound unfurled a long forgotten warmth in her. Having Tyler half naked in her kitchen was too cozy for her peace of mind.

"Would you mind putting on some clothes?" Her question rushed out, full of exasperation.

He glanced down at himself, then back at her. "Did I lose my sweatpants somewhere between the guest room and kitchen?"

She dumped a dirty bowl in the water, and a splash of suds leaped to the floor. "No, but I'd appreciate it if you'd put on a T-shirt."

"No shirt, no service, huh?"

How could he act so casual when she was coiled as tight as a spring? Wiping her hands on a dish towel, she faced him from the other side of the kitchen table and leveled a serious look on him.

"Tyler, I have a young son upstairs who will probably wake up within the next hour. He'll be shocked to find a strange man in the house, let alone one who's half naked." She moved to the spices sitting on the counter to put them away. "If you're going to insist on staying in the main house, you're going to have to use more discretion." For her own racing-out-of-control heart as much for propriety's sake.

"Yes, ma'am," Tyler relented. He could have added that the house was half his, so he had every right to run around completely naked in *his* half if he chose to, but remained quiet.

He watched her stretch to put a tin of baking powder on a high shelf. Her shirt lifted with the movement, exposing clingy pants that outlined the curve of her bottom and firm thighs. Desire rolled through him in heated waves, spurring him across the kitchen.

She spun around, watching him warily. "What?"

He smiled. "You have flour on your nose." He lifted his hand to wipe the smudge away.

She sucked in a swift breath and placed her palms on his chest to hold him back. Her hands were cool and soft against his flesh. When she would have pulled them away, he clasped her wrists, prolonging the torture.

Brianne tugged at the bonds imprisoning her hands, shivering at the way his heart thudded wildly beneath her palm. "Dammit, Tyler, stop toying with me."

His gaze bored into hers. "It's still there, isn't it?"

Brianne wanted to play stupid, but it was so painfully obvious the spark was still there, even after nine long years. "Yes," she whispered.

"Did you feel it with Boyd, too?" He stroked his thumb across the pulse in her wrist, and she trembled. "Did you quiver whenever *he* touched you?"

"Tyler, don't." They'd only end up hurting each other with this discussion. And she didn't particularly want to relive the embittered years with Boyd. Closing her eyes, she summoned the will to be strong. "*Please* go put on a shirt!"

Disgusted with himself for caring about Brianne's feelings for his half-brother, Tyler released her. A surge of old bitterness reminded him who she'd ultimately chosen, and everything she'd accumulated as a result.

With that thought in mind, he turned and left the kitchen.

Upstairs, he retrieved clean clothes and his shaving bag and went into the bathroom. As hot water pounded the tense muscles across his shoulders, he attempted to convince himself the only thing he was interested in was his inheritance. He wanted to make a respected name as a reining trainer in conjunction with Whitmore Acres. Just as it should have been years ago.

Twenty minutes later he emerged, showered, shaven, hair damp and combed back, and changed into a pair of jeans and a beige chambray shirt. Rolling up his sleeves, he went back down to the kitchen, feeling more civilized and refreshed.

The morning sun streamed through the window over the sink, brightening the room and promising another warm summer day. A sweet aroma mingled with the hickory scent of fried bacon, making his stomach growl. Brianne cast him a brief look, but said nothing as she pulled plates and bowls from the cupboard and set them at the table before returning to the stove.

Tyler located a mug from one of the cupboards and poured himself a cup of hot coffee. Leaning against the counter, he watched Brianne divide her attention between the pancakes she'd just poured on the hot griddle, and retrieving the butter, syrup, and a big bowl of fresh-cut peaches from the refrigerator. She placed the items on the table, along with the platter of bacon, and returned to flip the pancakes.

Tyler took a drink of coffee, savoring the strong flavor. He didn't miss the way she wouldn't look at him, even though he stood within touching distance. Well, he was certain he was about to rouse her attention.

"So, do you run the ranch now?" he asked conversationally.

Brianne stiffened at Tyler's oh-so-casually-asked question, then forced herself to relax. Being gone as long as he had, and knowing that Boyd and Landon were dead, Tyler would obviously be curious as to the ranch's status. "Yes," she replied, treading carefully with her answer. "I'm involved in all aspects of the business."

"Like a good owner should be." His tone held a trace of derision.

"Yes," she said defensively. She considered herself a damn good manager.

He lifted the mug to his lips, his expression unreadable. After a moment he asked, "Are you involved in the breeding?"

"I do the scheduling and negotiating, though I have Jasper and Steven, another trainer here on the ranch, help with the actual breeding." She placed the golden pancakes on top of the others stacked on the plate by the stove. "I also manage the finances, the selling and purchasing of the stock, and I oversee the employees."

He looked impressed. "You've become quite the businesswoman."

"I've worked hard." Catching the sound of her own curt tone, Brianne sighed to release her building frustration. The relaxation technique didn't work.

A ghost of a smile touched Tyler's mouth. "Is Whitmore Acres still only breeding quarter horses for cutting?"

She recalled the reining operation Tyler had managed before he'd left, and how it nearly dragged the ranch under. "Yes." Her answer was as brusque as her previous one. She didn't want to talk about the ranch anymore.

He didn't seem to notice. "Ever thought of broadening the ranch's breeding program?"

To include reining again? she wondered. "No. I don't have the extra finances to expand."

"Maybe you ought to think about taking on a partner."

Brianne met his gaze. He stared expectantly, waiting for her reply. It was on the tip of her tongue to say she didn't need a partner, when in fact she didn't because she already had one. He just didn't know it yet. Or did he?

After that double-edged comment of his, she knew she could no longer postpone the unavoidable discussion of his inheritance, not without lying or giving him some half-truth, which she refused to do. "Tyler—"

At that moment, Daniel came flying into the kitchen, his blond hair damp and combed away from his lightly freckled face. "Mom, can I take Fiero out riding—" Her son's words skidded to an abrupt halt, as did his booted feet, when he spotted Tyler. His dark blue gaze narrowed, filling with instant suspicion.

Oxygen came in short supply for Brianne as father and son took stock of each other; Tyler in interest, and Daniel with unconcealed wariness. Brianne wished the reunion could have been different, but she'd made a lot of wishes in her lifetime. Most hadn't come true.

"Who's this?" Daniel asked, glancing at her.

Brianne removed the pancakes from the griddle before they burned, her hand shaking. "Daniel, this is your..." She swallowed the word *father,* and forced out, "Uncle Tyler."

Daniel glared. "You're...my *dad's* brother?"

Tyler understood the boy's initial wariness. He was a stranger, after all. But the animosity in his tone was another matter altogether, and something he didn't feel he deserved. "Yes. Your father was my half-brother."

"How come I never heard of you before?" he asked suspiciously.

Tyler glanced at Brianne, his brow raised. "Yes, how come?"

Ignoring Tyler's question, Brianne approached her son, wanting to soothe the frown lines above his brow. She ached for him and knew he was thinking if Tyler was Boyd's brother then he'd probably be just as mean and heartless as Boyd had been.

She gave his shoulders a squeeze. "Daniel, it's true. This is your uncle Tyler. He left before you were born. I wasn't sure if he was ever coming back, so I never mentioned him." And anytime Tyler's name was mentioned, Boyd had flown into a rage. She'd learned early on in her marriage that Tyler was a subject not to be discussed. Unless Boyd instigated it, which usually happened after a night out drinking when he came home in a surly disposition, itching for a fight.

Daniel shrugged away and went to the refrigerator. He dismissed the whole incident by ignoring them all. Understanding his confusion, Brianne left him alone. As for Tyler, he looked totally bewildered by Daniel's attitude.

Not wanting to answer the silent questions in Tyler's eyes regarding her son's behavior, she cleared her throat and said, "Why don't we sit down and start breakfast?"

Tyler poured himself another cup of coffee and took a place at the table. Daniel, quiet and brooding, sat in the seat furthest from Tyler. Brianne made another platter of pancakes, then joined them, although she couldn't eat much for the knot in her stomach. Breakfast was an uncomfortable and awkward event. For a nine-year separation, Brianne had very little to contribute in way of casual conversation, and neither did Tyler, it seemed. Instead, he attempted to draw Daniel into a verbal exchange, but the boy's answers were curt and didn't invite further conversation.

When Daniel was done eating, he scooted his chair back with a loud scrape on the linoleum floor. "I'm going outside."

Brianne let him go, even though it was his job to clear the table. Today she'd excuse him, because she knew what he was going through emotionally.

With a sigh, she stood and began stacking dishes.

Tyler helped Brianne clear the table. "The boy seems old for his age."

Tyler's comment zapped through Brianne. The dishes in her hands rattled as she lowered them into the soapy water. She'd expected an idle remark about Daniel's hostile attitude. But an observation about Daniel's age made her more than a little nervous.

"Yes," she answered, wiping the table so she didn't have to meet Tyler's gaze. Daniel *was* wise beyond his years, and much too serious.

Tyler refilled both their cups with fresh hot coffee. "How old is he?"

Brianne dropped the sponge in the sink, her body flashing hot and cold at the same time. Heart pounding wildly in her chest, she faced him. She wondered if he somehow knew Daniel was his and was testing her for the truth.

"He's eight," she forced out, the word sticking in her throat.

A bitter smile curved Tyler's mouth, and disdain reflected in his dark eyes. "You sure didn't waste any time with Boyd, did you?"

He believed Daniel was Boyd's. Equal shares of relief and anger washed over her at his caustic remark, drowning out the fear.

Curbing the impulse to strike back with a searing

comment of her own regarding his abandonment, she rerouted her thoughts to a safer topic. "I thought you might want to know how your father and Boyd died."

Tyler scrubbed a hand over his jaw, mentally kicking himself for his cutting remark to Brianne. But, damn, he resented that she'd married Boyd so quickly after he'd left and had obviously secured her future as a Whitmore by getting pregnant immediately. She was a smarter businesswoman than he would have given her credit for. Why would she take the bastard son when she could have the real thing?

Determined to keep his grudges under wraps, and wanting to dissolve some of the tension in the room, he sighed heavily and sat down. "What happened to Landon?"

She slid into the seat across from him. Reaching for the coffee he'd poured, she added a splash of cream. Her expression softened for the news she was about to deliver.

"He died of lung cancer seven years ago," she said, her eyes filling with sadness. "He found out shortly after you left. The cancer was so pervasive, they only gave him a few months to live. But he hung on longer than his doctor predicted."

Glancing away, Tyler tamped the sorrow engulfing him, wondering if Landon had tried to hang on, hoping he'd return before he died. The thought tore at him, adding to his guilt.

"What about Boyd?" he asked, once his emotions were controlled.

Brianne wrapped her hands around her mug and stared into the depths of her coffee. She suppressed a shiver as his question thrust her back three years in time. She hated recalling the awful night Boyd died, his excessive drinking, the nasty accusations, the fury of Tyler inheriting half of a ranch that should have been solely his.

Swallowing the tangle of emotion rising in her throat, she lifted her gaze to Tyler's. "He'd been drinking one night and drove his truck into a tree." Tracing a pattern on the wooden table with her finger, she detached herself from the turmoil of that night. "He wasn't wearing a seat belt. The sheriff said he was killed instantly."

"I'm sorry," Tyler said softly, and with genuine regret. "I wish I'd been here..."

"You would have been notified of your father's death, and Boyd's, if anyone had known where you were." Censure vibrated in her voice.

"Doesn't seem like you tried too hard to find me."

"We *did* try and find you! Landon instructed his attorneys to locate you, but every lead turned up a dead end. You drifted so often that no one could keep track of you!"

Tyler couldn't refute that fact—that's exactly what the private investigator had told him.

Brianne's mouth thinned in reproach. "Besides, I shouldn't have had to find *you*."

Her insinuation made him bristle, prompting him to strike back with his own accusation. "You damn well should have tried harder, considering you have something that belongs to me."

She met his gaze, and the fear there stunned him.

He swore, tired of avoiding the real issues. "When were you planning on telling me about my half of the inheritance?" he demanded. "Or were you just going to wait and see if I'd just dropped by to say 'hi,' then be on my way?"

Brianne shivered at Tyler's thunderous expression and the way he leaned over the table toward her, hands fisted on the smooth, wooden surface. "Of course I was going to tell you about your inheritance," she said defensively. "But I'm still trying to deal with the fact that you're here after all these years, Tyler."

The corner of his mouth curled into a parody of a smile. "Well, let me save you from worrying what you should do. I've got a letter from Landon's attorney stating half the ranch is mine. I want it."

Feeling provoked and cornered, Brianne shot out of her chair, recklessly coming around to his side of the table. "My, aren't *you* suddenly the responsible one!" she mocked, gaining satisfaction when his jaw clenched at her well-aimed taunt. "You didn't seem very concerned about the ranch these past *nine* years." *When I learned your brother had siphoned the finances dry... When I was struggling to keep the house and operation from going into bankruptcy... When I was fighting to hold on to the Whitmore legacy for Daniel.*

White-hot anger blazed in his dark eyes. "I want what's mine."

Pacing away from him, she released a breath that drained her fury of moments before. Determined to be civil and settle the issue fairly, she turned to face him.

"Look, Tyler," she began rationally. "The truth about your inheritance is that you're paper rich but cash poor."

"Paper rich but cash poor?" Skepticism lined his features. "What the hell are you talking about?"

"The ranch is bringing in a steady income, enough to pay the bills and still generate a good amount of revenue, but there isn't a huge chunk of money sitting in the bank," she explained. "Eighty percent of the profits go right back into the ranch."

"Sounds like smart business to me." His scowl deepened, lining his features with impatience. "What are you getting at, Brianne?"

She forced a bright smile. "I've been running the place for three years. There's no reason why I can't keep managing the ranch."

He stood and slowly approached her, looking dark and dangerous. Brianne's heart responded with a distinct "thump" in her chest. She stepped back, wedging herself into the corner of the counter.

"I'll protect your portion of the ranch and look out for your best interests while you're gone," she rushed to assure him.

"How convenient." He rested his hands on the counter on either side of her. His forearms pressed into her waist. "I have to admit your suggestion sounds very...reasonable."

"Of course it's reasonable!" She inched back, but there was no room left to escape. "And I'll do everything I can to ensure the growth of your inheritance."

"Of course you would." A smile tipped his mouth, belying the blue flames burning in his eyes. "That would be the ideal situation, wouldn't it, Bree? You running the ranch without me underfoot to stir up trouble?"

She shook her head and opened her mouth to say something, but Tyler pressed his fingers over her lips.

"I have no intention of moving on," he told her. "And don't bother trying to talk me out of it."

"I wasn't." The denial was muffled by his fingers.

"You were." He removed his fingers, letting the tips slide over her jaw in a brazen caress. "I've got plans for Whitmore Acres. Everything will go a lot smoother if I have your cooperation."

"Dammit, Tyler, you have no right to expect anything from me! You've been gone nine years. Not once did you have the decency to write or call and let me know you were okay!"

"I saw no need to once you married Boyd." His tone

held an edge of disdain. He shoved away from her. Halfway across the kitchen he spun back around. "You promised to marry *me*, Brianne, remember?"

She sucked in a painful breath, her heart swelling with all the memories. Oh, yes, she remembered. The sweet promises. The heartbreak. The despair.

"You left with no word, Tyler. Nothing!" And when days had turned into weeks, she'd believed Boyd when he'd told her Tyler wouldn't be coming back. After all, Tyler hadn't contacted her.

"Doesn't seem like you missed me too much. I wasn't even gone six weeks and you married Boyd."

"I had no..." *Choice,* she thought, but caught the word before it escaped. How could she explain how alone and afraid she'd been when she'd learned she was an unwed, pregnant eighteen-year-old with no future for her child? That *he'd* left her with little choice but the ones she'd made. When she'd turned to her father for help and support, he'd scorned her, thinning her meager options. And when she'd confided in Boyd that she was pregnant, he'd offered her the only solution to her predicament.

Yes, out of desperation she'd married Boyd, but not without a steep price that cost more than just her pride.

"You had no what, Bree?" Tyler prompted. "No one to warm your bed? You had no heritage but a drunk for a father and the ranch started looking mighty good? You've come a long way, Ms. Taylor-Whitmore, from living in a rundown shack in a bad neighborhood to owning half of Whitmore Acres. I guess it's just a matter of sleeping with the *right* Whitmore."

Brianne wrapped her arms around her waist to keep from trembling, or reaching out and slapping him. His words were sharper than a blade, cutting all the way to her soul and leaving everything in between in fine shreds. When she dared to meet his gaze, fearing the worst recriminations from him, she discovered instead a hurt to match her own.

She turned toward the counter, not wanting to delve deeper into this discussion for the pain and secrets they'd end up unearthing. The past was the past. Justifying her reasons for her hasty marriage to Boyd wouldn't change all the hurt between them. She didn't think anything would ever bridge that gap.

Doing her best to ignore the crushing pressure in her chest, she concentrated on the shortbread squares that needed to be wrapped in cellophane. Methodically, she tore a strip of plastic wrap from the box and piled the squares in the center.

Tyler pushed his fingers through his hair, the movement jerky and agitated. He hadn't meant for their conversation to get so heated. But he couldn't retrieve the damaging words, and he couldn't bring himself to apologize, either. Everything he'd said was true; she hadn't bothered to deny any of it.

They couldn't continue throwing the past at one another or they'd kill each other with the spiked barbs before a week was out.

Business, Tyler. Stick to business.

Dropping to his chair, he leaned forward, bracing his elbows on his knees. "Were there any stipulations in Landon's will?" he asked in an attempt to get things back on track.

She continued with her task, not looking at him. "There were none. Half the ranch is legally yours." Rinsing her hands, she grabbed the dish towel and faced him. Resignation, and the remnants of the pain he'd caused with his careless statements shimmered in her gaze. "I'll call Jed tomorrow and make an appointment for you to see him regarding your portion of the estate."

They were back to a civil, if not guarded truce. "Thank you. I'd like to get everything settled as soon as possible."

She nodded, and they stared at one another for long minutes, the ticking of the clock on the wall the only sound breaking the thick silence enveloping the room.

"Were you hoping I wouldn't come back?" Tyler asked recklessly, risking the fragile treaty for a question he already knew the answer to, but needed to ask nonetheless.

"Yes," Brianne whispered, twisting the terry towel in her hands. But not for the reasons he believed, that she wanted the ranch all to herself.

She was more worried about Daniel, and her own vulnerable heart.

CHAPTER THREE

JASPER RAWLINGS barged into the kitchen minutes after Brianne and Tyler's standoff, his gaze searching the kitchen. His hazel eyes brightened when he spotted Tyler, and a wide smile split his tanned, weathered face beneath the brim of an ancient leather hat.

"Well, I'll be damned!" Jasper exclaimed, his bow-legged gait carrying him across the kitchen to Tyler. "I thought Daniel was just making up stories about an Uncle Tyler being here. Wait until the Missus hears about this! Betty'll split her seams!"

Tyler greeted him with a firm shake of his hand that turned into a masculine bear hug. They broke apart, and Tyler grinned at the man who'd been an integral part of Whitmore Acres for over thirty years. "Jasper, you haven't changed a bit."

Jasper scoffed at that, blinking away the sudden moisture gathering in his eyes. Examining Tyler at arm's length, he shook his head in disbelief. "I heard we had us a guest. I just didn't believe it was really you. Welcome home, Tyler."

"Thanks. It's good to be home."

Brianne stepped forward, springing at the chance to be rid of Tyler for a while. "Jasper, would you mind helping Tyler get his horse settled in? I'd do it myself, but I've got my hands full here today."

"Don't you worry 'bout a thing, Miss Brianne. It'd be my pleasure." He stared at Tyler. "I can't believe you're really back. You must've heard about your inheritance."

He glanced at Brianne. "That had something to do with it."

"Well, no matter the reason," Jasper said, tugging on his leather hat. "I should be skinnin' your hide for bein' gone so long, but I'm just so damned happy you're back that I can't bring myself to. Now let's go make that horse of yours comfortable." He headed toward the screen door.

Tyler followed. Just when Brianne thought she was finally going to be granted a few hours' respite, he stopped at the door and met her gaze.

"We'll talk more later."

She didn't doubt it.

Needing fresh air and someone to talk to other than all the males surrounding her on a daily basis, Brianne grabbed a care package of goodies and headed toward Jasper and Betty's place, located a short, half-mile distance from her house.

Betty was the closest thing she had to a mother, and Brianne loved the older woman as if she were her own kin. Her own mother had died when she'd been a little girl, and when her father, Curtis, had come to work for Landon, bringing her along during the summertime and weekends, Betty had taken her under her wing and given her the feminine nurturing and guidance she'd been lacking. Betty and Jasper couldn't have children, but Betty had confided that between Brianne, Tyler, and Boyd, she'd been surrounded by enough youngins to ease the emptiness of not having her own offspring. And she loved and treated Daniel like the grandchild she'd never have.

Seeing Betty standing at the kitchen window, Brianne opened the back screen door and entered the small, com-

pact kitchen, a homey place where she always seemed
to find the comfort she craved.

She hoped today was no exception.

Betty turned from the chopping block next to the sink
where she was slicing carrots for the stew simmering on
the stove. Nearing her mid-sixties, Betty was plump and
healthy with pale blue eyes full of wisdom. She always
wore her blond-turned-gray hair up in a bun on her head,
along with a warm and welcoming smile that lit up her
entire face.

"Hi, Betty," Brianne said, the greeting escaping on a
sigh as weary as the smile on her lips.

The other woman dropped the carrots into the pot and
lowered the flame to let the stew simmer. "Hi, yourself,
dear," she said, wiping her hands on the apron tied
around her ample waist.

"I just wanted to drop these off," Brianne said, in-
dicating the plastic-covered plate in her hand, knowing
she'd stopped by for so much more. "I know how much
Jasper likes my raspberry shortbread squares. He was
eyeballing them this morning, and I've got plenty to
spare."

"Been baking, have you?" Betty said, amusement
twinkling in her eyes. Taking the baked goods from
Brianne, she set it on the kitchen counter. "Would
Tyler's sudden appearance be the reason?"

The older woman knew her too well. Grinning wryly,
Brianne sank into one of the wooden chairs at the
kitchen table. "Word travels fast around here."

"He's already come by." Always seeming to know
what Brianne needed, whether it be her special blend of
raspberry tea or a listening ear, Betty filled a teakettle
with water and set it on a back burner to boil, then sat
across from her. "He sure has grown into a handsome
man."

Brianne couldn't refute that. Tyler had filled out over the years, his body honed to muscular perfection by hard, physical labor. Having seen him half naked, having been trapped between him and a counter and having touched that powerful chest with her own hands, she could confirm the latent strength beneath his warm, firm flesh. And she'd bet that slow, easy grin of his had broken a few hearts over the years, just as he'd broken hers.

"Has he seen Daniel?" Betty asked conversationally, though there was a deeper level of curiosity in her gaze that made Brianne extremely uncomfortable.

"Yes," she replied evenly. "Though I can't say Daniel is too pleased to discover he's got an uncle."

Betty nodded her head in understanding. "Considering what the boy went through with Boyd, give him some time to come around."

"I'd rather he didn't form a close bond with his uncle," she said, her tone sharper than she'd intended. That damn fear always crept up when she least expected it.

Betty arched a brow. The kettle whistled and she stood, her gaze locking with Brianne's. "Seems to me Daniel could use a male influence in his life."

"Daniel has Jasper, and Steven—"

"Someone *blood* related, who'd have his best interests at heart," Betty said meaningfully, then moved toward the stove.

Brianne stared at Betty's broad back as she prepared two mugs of her raspberry tea. She'd always wondered if Betty had suspected the truth about Daniel's parentage. No one had ever questioned her claim of Daniel being born two months premature, but a woman's mind was a bit sharper than a man's when it came to pregnancies.

"Tyler is hardly a stable role model for my son," she said in her defense. And Tyler's only interest at the moment was his half of the ranch, and making her life miserable.

Betty set two steaming cups of tea on the table, and took her place across from Brianne. "Now what would make you say that?"

Brianne wrapped her hand around the ceramic mug, absorbing the warmth. "Because I'm certain he's leaving soon." She didn't know yet *how* she was going to get him off a ranch that was half his, but she was determined to find a way before he had a chance to be any kind of influence to her son, or exert his newfound authority in running a ranch that had been operating just fine without him.

"I find it hard to believe that Tyler would give up his half of the ranch so easily," Betty said.

Oh, she was certain there would be a battle, but she was used to fighting for her livelihood. Boyd had taught her well in the ways of self-preservation.

Brianne blew on her tea, then took a sip. "Considering how difficult it was for Landon's attorneys to locate Tyler, it doesn't seem he stays in one place long enough to call home. It's just a matter of time before he leaves." Even if it took an extra incentive for him to move on, she thought.

"Tyler belongs here," Betty said, her voice quiet, but firm. "Having Tyler at Whitmore Acres is what Landon ultimately wanted."

Brianne frowned. Betty was supposed to be supporting *her* side of the ranch, not the enemy's. "It might be what Landon wanted, but I'm sure once the novelty of working such a small operation wears off and Tyler gets restless, he'll move on to something more exciting."

Betty reached across the table and patted Brianne's arm, the gesture more sympathetic than comforting. "I guess only time will tell."

Time, Brianne hoped, would prove Betty wrong—that Tyler was just as unreliable as he'd been nine years ago.

Whitmore Acres had been well cared for. From what Tyler discovered from Jasper while they worked together getting Sweet Justice settled in a private paddock, Brianne was the sole reason the ranch was thriving. She ran a tight operation, and Jasper assured him that she was as ruthless as any man when negotiating business. The strong, confident woman Tyler was coming to know was a direct contradiction to the vulnerable, insecure girl he'd left behind.

Jasper lightly touched on Boyd and his wild ways that had nearly taken the ranch under. The topic disgusted the old man so that he only pursed his lips and shook his head, muttering, "That boy could've had it all, but he was so bitter that he nearly destroyed everything your pappy worked so hard to build."

Jasper's comment settled heavily on Tyler and made him question his own buried bitterness. He didn't want his resentment of the past to interfere with his plans for the future.

Jasper gave him a tour of the facilities. He met Steven, a nice young man who helped Jasper train the horses. The ranch wasn't as grand or stocked as it once had been when Landon was alive, but the place was immaculately maintained. The two large buildings housing the stables, the barn, the breeding shed, and the huge lighted indoor arena used in the winter months for training had been recently painted and renovated. The security system had been upgraded, the box stalls newly insulated. A horse, or trainer, couldn't ask for more pleasurable accommodations.

Outside, the large paddocks were secure, the pastures green, and all the horses healthy and well tended by the grooms Brianne employed. A separate fenced-in area housed over fifty head of Herefords used to train the horses to cut.

The condition of the facilities pleased him, along with the knowledge that there was still plenty of space to expand to once again include a reining program. To restore his dream that had been shattered so long ago.

Leaning his elbows on the top railing of the white fencing circling the paddocks, Tyler stared at the magnificent animals and nature's beauty surrounding him. He absorbed it all, reveling in the fact that half belonged to him. A sense of contentment filled him, triggering regret for all the years he'd wasted drifting from place to place.

He glanced at his wristwatch, stunned to realize it was nearly five o'clock. The whole afternoon had passed quickly, and he hadn't even familiarized himself with the actual business end of the ranch; the books, the breeding schedule, their customers. He had the rest of his life, he told himself, and smiled at how good that sounded.

Following the gravel path back to the main house, he decided most importantly he needed to secure Brianne's confidence if he wanted to gain her support to expand the breeding program. Things would go much smoother for them as business partners if she didn't fight him every inch of the way. Which, after speaking with Jasper, he sensed she'd do.

That meant putting past differences aside and being civil with one another. He could manage the feat if she could.

The two-story structure he'd grown up in was simple in appearance, but solidly built to last decades of harsh winters and scorching summers. Tyler jogged up the steps leading to the wide veranda, wondering where

Daniel had disappeared to. He'd seen him earlier riding his chestnut, Fiero. The boy hadn't said two words to him since he'd left the kitchen that morning. Tyler chalked up the boy's animosity to having his "Uncle Tyler" poaching on his territory.

He stepped through the front door. The interior of the house was cool and quiet, except for an occasional hum filtering from the back room downstairs. Tyler followed the noise and found Brianne sitting in front of a sewing machine. Her forehead was creased in concentration as she guided a panel of floral material through the hammering needle.

Leaning his shoulder against the jamb, Tyler smiled, watching her maneuver the cloth with practiced ease. She'd pulled back the sheers covering the window. Sunlight spilled into the femininely decorated room, touching on her braided hair. For an instant, he imagined her hair loose, the blond, silken strands tumbling over her shoulders in soft waves, just as it had been that summer afternoon when he'd kissed her for the first time. He'd foolishly thought one passionate kiss would be enough to quell the desire she kindled within him. Instead, he'd been drugged by the taste of her, intoxicated by her softness, and aroused by her open response.

Tyler's chest tightened at the memories. He'd never meant to touch her back then. At twenty-three he'd known it was wrong to get involved with an eighteen-year-old, or to take advantage of her vulnerability. But she'd been so soft and warm, so sweetly responsive that he'd fallen hard. And he'd wanted so desperately to protect her from a father who turned abusive when he drank.

As a kid of eight Brianne had followed Tyler around like a puppy while her father, Curtis, worked on the ranch as a trainer. At the time Brianne's devotion had irritated him. She was, after all, nothing but a pesky taga-long. But as the years melted away and she blossomed into a beautiful young woman, he found himself attracted to her when he knew he shouldn't be. After Landon fired Curtis for drinking on the job, a habit Landon had been repeatedly lenient with but could no longer risk harm to his animals, Brianne had sought refuge in the horses and ranch. She'd used the stables as a hideaway from her father, not going home until late, when she knew he'd be passed out for the night.

Then one day Tyler found her by the creek crying. He'd seen the discoloration on her cheek, knew Curtis had hit her, and wanted to kill the man. She'd begged him to leave her father alone. She'd claimed Curtis didn't know what he was doing, that he still missed her mother, Sarah, and didn't know how to cope with the loss. Then she'd curled into his lap and asked him to hold her. He had, stroking her back and murmuring soothing words. When she'd lifted her lips to his, her eyes huge and shimmering with need, he'd given in to temptation and kissed her.

They'd made love a couple of weeks after that first kiss. He'd wanted to marry her. She'd happily agreed. They'd talked about living on the ranch, and having babies. Lots of babies. Things had been sweet that summer, idyllic, until Boyd had destroyed every dream Tyler ever had. And Brianne had married the brother with all the riches.

Yes, she was a smart businesswoman.

Shaking off the memories before they dragged him under, Tyler cleared his throat. She started at the sound and jerked her head toward him.

She pulled the pins from her pursed lips and dropped them in a plastic container beside the sewing machine. "Tyler," she exclaimed. "I didn't hear you come in."

He wasn't about to tell her he'd been standing there

for the past five minutes reminiscing about their past. "What are you doing?" he asked in an attempt to keep the conversation light.

Lifting the material from her lap, she examined the stitches she'd made, then tacked a piece of fabric with a pin before looking at him. "I'm making a dress."

"Seems like a pretty fancy outfit for mucking out stalls," he said in a teasing drawl.

To his surprise she blushed. "It's for a dance next month," she explained, ducking her head to her project once again. "Did you get your mare settled?"

"Yes." He walked into the room, her soft feminine scent wreaking havoc on his senses. Running his callused fingers over a bolt of silky material, he smiled. "I think Sweet Justice will fit in with the rest of the horses just fine."

Brianne eyed him warily. "Why are you being so nice?"

He laughed, amused at her cautious expression. He supposed his new attitude was abrupt, considering their earlier hostility. "You're making me feel like a villain in a bad Western movie."

Standing, she crossed to the other end of the room to drape the half-sewn dress over the dressmaker's form. "This morning you acted like one."

"I agree things got heated and I probably said some things I shouldn't have. If you're looking for an apology I don't have one."

"Of course not." She looked over her shoulder at him, hurt in her eyes. "What would you ever have to be sorry for?"

He should have known she wouldn't make this easy. "Look, Brianne, despite how things have gone so far, I didn't come back so we could fight. I only want what's rightfully mine, which I think we've already established.''

"Very clearly,'' she said in a sharp tone.

He sighed and shoved his fingers through his hair. "Since I'm going to be a part of Whitmore Acres, I think it would be best if you and I try to get along, for everyone's sake.''

She fussed with the collar and sleeves on the dress. "Fine.''

"Truce?'' He held out his hand. His gaze dared her to take it as a way of sealing their agreement.

Brianne shook his hand while crossing the fingers of her other hand behind her back. "Truce,'' she muttered. She refused to let down *all* her shields with this man.

His smile was slow and lazy. "That wasn't so difficult, now was it?''

She returned his smile with a stiff one of her own. "Not at all.''

"Good.'' He sat on the peach and mint green cushion nestled in the cove of the window seat. The direct contrast of her feminine frills made him look more virile and masculine than he had a right to. "Now that that's settled, I wanted to talk to you about my half of the inheritance.''

She tensed. She didn't want to discuss business until she figured out what to do about Tyler, and the ranch. She didn't want him dabbling in the business she'd labored to rebuild with nothing more than the couple hundred dollars she'd gotten by selling her beat-up Toyota after Boyd died. Dammit, the ranch was all she had, and all she had to offer Daniel!

"What?'' she said, striving for a flippancy she didn't feel as she reached for a pin and began tucking the hem of the dress. "You want to split the property directly down the middle? You take the east side and I'll take the west?"

"That would be the ideal solution," he agreed, picking up a lace pillow and absently fingering the ruffled edge. "But not very realistic. I want to be involved in all aspects of the business. I want to review the books."

The bombshell dropped, splintering Brianne's nerves. The hand dipping into the pin box jerked, and the container leaped off the shelf. Pins scattered everywhere on the hardwood floor. She cursed her clumsiness even as her mind conjured a plausible excuse to put Tyler off.

"You...can't," she blurted, then cringed at the desperation threading her voice.

He lifted a brow. "Why? Do you have something to hide?"

"Of course not!" A heated blush crept over her face. She swept up as many pins as she could with her hands, wincing as they poked her fingers. She just wasn't ready for this!

She met his gaze, wishing she could read his mind and knew what he intended. "I, uh, just sent them to the accountant to give me a quarterly review. I do have a fairly recent financial if you'd like to see that."

"That would be a good start, and then we can go from there."

She straightened, a tremulous smile lifting her lips. "Fine. I should have the journals back from the accountant in a week or so," she said, buying herself time.

He nodded shortly. "That works for me."

"Great." Her thoughts were so scattered she couldn't think straight, let alone attempt even stitches. "I, uh, should get dinner on the table."

"I'll go wash up."

They met back in the kitchen a few minutes later. Tyler helped himself to a glass of iced tea and sat at the table while Brianne popped biscuits in the oven to warm. She dished up the carrots and potatoes from the Crock-Pot and placed the roast on the platter, trying not to think about the financials she'd promised Tyler.

Daniel came into the kitchen, cast a brief look at Tyler, and slid into an empty chair across from him. A few minutes later everyone was seated and supper was being served. The only sound in the room was the clatter of utensils against dishes and the occasional request to pass an entrée.

"I saw you riding your horse today, Daniel," Tyler commented as he heaped potatoes on his plate, then passed the bowl to Brianne. "You handle him well."

Stabbing a slice of carrot with his fork, Daniel glared at Tyler with turbulent blue eyes. "So?"

The kid didn't give an inch, Tyler thought, ladling gravy over his roast and potatoes. "So, I was thinking maybe you might be interested in learning the process of breaking and training the horses."

"Don't you think Daniel's kind of young for that?" Brianne asked tightly.

"No." Tyler leveled a steady look at her. Fear flashed in her eyes, but he didn't understand its source. "Landon started teaching me as soon as I learned to ride a horse."

Daniel pushed his food around on his plate. "Why would you want to waste your time teaching me?" A hint of insecurity seeped through his hostility, but he still held his chin high, not quite ready to yield to the idea.

"I don't think it would be a waste. You're young and smart. Starting early would give you an advantage." He smiled to put the boy at ease.

Daniel's gaze flickered to Brianne uncertainly, then back to Tyler. "Yeah, well, I don't have time for that."

"I understand. Let me know if you change your mind." Tyler guessed what the boy didn't have time for was him. And he was determined to find out *why*.

CHAPTER FOUR

"MIND if I join you?" Tyler stepped onto the dark veranda and shut the screen door.

Brianne pushed the porch swing into action with the toe of her shoe, hesitating to answer.

"I promise I won't bite." He moved toward her, the soft light filtering out the living room window silhouetting his large build. "Truce, remember?"

Yes, she remembered, though it changed nothing between them. "I'd rather be alone."

"I'm sure you would, but we've got a lot of things to catch up on." The swing creaked a protest as he settled his weight on the opposite end.

"Such as?"

"Such as… Do you have a boyfriend I need to know about?"

She gave him an incredulous look, unable to believe he'd be so bold as to ask such a question. "If I did, it wouldn't be any of your business or concern."

"If?" His tone was smug as he stretched his arm along the back of the swing and toyed with her braid. "I'll take that as a no."

Annoyance rippled through her, along with a surge of heat where his fingers brushed her shoulder. "I've dated a few men, but I'm not serious with anyone, if that's what you're prying for."

"Just curious," he murmured.

Just as curious as she was about him. Grasping her braid, she pulled the tail end out of his reach while idly torturing herself with thoughts of how many women he'd been through in the time he'd been gone. He could have married someone else, for all she knew.

Slipping the elastic band off the end of her braid, she began separating the strands. "How about you, Tyler? Do *you* have a girlfriend or wife I should worry about showing up out of the blue?" Her tone was light, humorous, but her insides twisted with emotions she didn't want to acknowledge.

Surprise entered his eyes before he replied, "No. No girlfriend, but I almost got married once…a long time ago." He gave her a reckless grin that lacked any real enthusiasm. "I've learned over the years that I'm not the committing kind."

"No, that doesn't seem to be one of your stronger suits, does it?" Her voice was a whisper, and Brianne could hardly believe the words had actually slipped out. "I'm sorry, Tyler, that comment was uncalled for." Propping the heels of her feet on the edge of the swing, she wrapped her arms around her up-drawn knees. "I know part of the reason why you left has to do with your father shutting down the reining operation—"

"Landon wasn't my *father*, Brianne," he interrupted. Abruptly, he stood and walked to the porch stairs, propping a shoulder on the side column. "I'm illegitimate, a bastard. I don't even know who my real father is, and my mother didn't stick around long enough to see me out of diapers."

Brianne hugged her knees tighter to keep from going to him and offering a little comfort. He stood with his fingers thrust into the front pockets of his jeans, his back ramrod straight. His expression was diamond-hard. A rebel stance, but beneath the facade she detected the pain and uncertainty of the confused man he'd been at twenty-three.

"I know Landon's not your real father, but he's the

man who raised you," she said of the kind, gentle man who'd been more a father to her than her own had been. "No matter what you believe, he loved you like you were his own son. That's as close to being a father as it gets, Tyler."

"He took the reining operation from me, without giving me a chance to defend it," he argued.

"The reining operation was losing money. Landon did what he thought was best for Whitmore Acres. His decision had nothing to do with you personally."

Boyd's vendetta to get him off the ranch had been *very* personal, Tyler thought. And he'd used Landon as a pawn in his spiteful game. But how could he tell Brianne about Boyd tampering with the books when he didn't have any proof to back his claim? All he had was a gut instinct honed from years of witnessing Boyd's conniving schemes.

"How do you know so much about what Landon thought?"

Brianne left the swing and braced her back against the column across from him. "Your father and I became very close in the two years I lived here before he died. He'd always planned to split everything between you and Boyd, and he never meant to drive you away. The night before he died, he told me he hoped the inheritance would bring you back to the ranch, where you belong."

"I'll bet that made Boyd real happy," Tyler commented derisively.

"Boyd was selfish. He never loved and respected the land and animals the way you did. He hated your close relationship with Landon, and he did everything in his power to hurt you." *Even offering to marry me when I'd been so alone and afraid…and pregnant with your child.*

Tyler gave a short, dry laugh. "Boyd always knew what buttons to push with me."

"Oh, Tyler," she sighed, the sound weary and sad. "Why didn't you come back, or at least call?"

He looked at her, staring deep. "I did come back."

Her eyes widened. "You did?"

He nodded and glanced away. "I was so angry at Landon for taking away the one thing I'd worked so hard for. I left the ranch, determined to make it on my own as a reining trainer and breeder. I wanted to prove Landon wrong and show him I could succeed. When I finally cooled down and decided to come back and talk to him rationally, it was too late."

She frowned. "Too late?"

"Yeah, too late." He pinned her with an unwavering look. "Ironically enough, I came back on the day you married Boyd, just in time to see the happy couple walk hand in hand down the courthouse steps."

"No," Brianne managed the denial, unable to believe fate could be so cruel. "I never knew. I thought you'd—" She swallowed the words "abandoned me," and said instead, "You should have come home, regardless of what you saw that day."

"I had nothing left to come back for."

"You had everything to come back for!" *Her. Daniel.* If only she hadn't believed Boyd when he'd told her Tyler wouldn't be coming back. If only she hadn't given in to her fear and insecurities and married Boyd. If only she'd waited one more day...

"Boyd had it all for a while, didn't he?" Tyler said, his mouth curling into a bitter smile. "He got the ranch and he got the girl. And the girl got the ranch."

Meeting Tyler's searching gaze, she steeled herself from the sadness and regret engulfing her. "Tyler, I don't want to talk about this. Arguing about the past isn't going to change any of it.''

Tyler released a long, low breath. "You're right," he agreed, his mood changing abruptly. Grabbing her hand, he tugged her down the stairs. "Come on.''

Brianne gasped and followed him. "Tyler, wait!" She stumbled on the last step. He easily steadied her, but didn't stop his stride.

She had to double her steps to keep up with his long legs. "Where are we going?" She wasn't frightened, only curious.

He glanced at her and smiled. An honest, warm smile full of pride. "There's someone very special I want you to meet."

Before she had a chance to question him, they slipped into the stable housing her mares. A single dim light in the back illuminated the interior enough to see where they were going. The scent of hay and horses and leather hung in the air, reassuring smells that relaxed her.

She followed him down the isle, suspecting the "special someone" was his horse. Automatically scanning the stalls, she checked on her horses. All seemed quiet and content except for the occasional soft nicker.

Tyler stopped at a stall and made a clicking sound with his tongue. The horse within strolled to the gate. Grinning, Tyler unlatched the closure and opened the gate, giving the horse a gentle rub on the nose.

"Brianne, I'd like you to meet Sweet Justice, or "Jussie," as I affectionately call her."

Delighted by the beauty of the bay, Brianne slowly stepped into the stall next to Tyler. A white blaze marked the horse's face. Brianne stroked her hand over Jussie's gleaming coat, and the animal's lean muscles quivered in response.

"Oh, Tyler, she's just beautiful," she breathed in appreciation.

"Thanks." Pride flowed through Tyler. He smiled, enjoying Brianne's gentle reverence with his mare.

Brianne's eyes danced with pleasure as she pet Sweet Justice, murmuring low, soothing words of praise to the horse. Jussie nudged her for more attention, and Brianne released a throaty laugh, a sexy, inviting sound that kicked Tyler's pulse into a heavy beat. Moonlight painted her features, highlighting the wet sheen of her lips and the creamy expanse of her throat.

Shifting close to Jussie, Tyler caressed his palm down the horse's neck. Idly, he wondered how Brianne's lips would feel beneath his, the taste and texture of her mouth. He shook off the arousing thoughts before they got him in trouble.

"She's so sweet, so gentle," Brianne commented, lavishing more affection on the mare.

"Don't let the docile act fool ya," Tyler replied with a grin. "She's as fast and powerful as a bullet when I want her to be. She's won her share of purse money in reining."

"Is that what you've been doing since you've been gone?" she asked curiously. "Competing?"

"I didn't start competing until about three years ago," Tyler said. "Bill, the man I worked for at the time, encouraged me to give it a try with one of his champion horses. After entering my first competition at a local rodeo I was hooked."

Brianne reached for a bucket of oats hanging just outside the door and hooked it on a peg in Jussie's stall. Grabbing a handful of the treat, she offered it to the mare. "How did you come across Sweet Justice?"

"I bought her from Bill when she was a foal." He shifted on his feet, suddenly restless in the small confines of the stall. Brianne's feminine scent filled his senses, even over the earthier smells of horse and hay.

Brianne laughed lightly as Jussie snorted into her palm, searching for more food. "Greedy wench," she murmured, brushing her fingertips over the animal's silky muzzle before dipping her hand into the pail again. "Do you train cutting horses anymore?" she asked Tyler.

His gaze captured hers in the sultry warmth of the night. The question was asked in an easy tone, but he got the feeling she was digging for deeper clues. "Right now I'm mainly concentrating on reining."

"Oh." Brianne glanced back at Jussie, frowning.

Leaning his shoulder against the wall, Tyler decided to touch on his plans for Whitmore Acres. "I'm thinking of acquiring a reining stud with strong bloodlines so I can breed Sweet Justice."

Wariness, and fear, flashed through her eyes. "You can breed Sweet Justice to one of my studs," she said slowly, almost cautiously, as if she wasn't sure she wanted to commit her studs to his mare, but felt obligated to issue the offer. "Caralon's Phantom and Desert Shadow are both excellent, healthy quarter horse studs."

"That would be fine if I was just interested in breeding and selling, but I want to train and show them, too. There's a champion reining stud I'm interested in."

"Really?" The one word was faint, her smile stiff.

Tyler nodded. He sensed Brianne's resistance, had anticipated it even. "He's Roman Warrior of Eckerly, and has excellent bloodlines."

Brianne smoothed her palm over Jussie's silky, warm coat. "Good bloodlines don't come cheap, Tyler."

"No, but the payoff is worth the cost," he argued mildly. "I plan to train the foal to show in its third year and eventually build up a good, solid line for pleasure and reining.''

Brianne took a calming breath, hating the anxiety choking her. ''We don't train the horses for show here.'' Her tone was firm, unyielding.

Tyler raised a brow. ''Whitmore Acres used to show the cutting *and* reining horses.''

The challenge in his tone made her nervous. ''And you saw for yourself just how *unsuccessful* the reining operation was,'' she said, slipping out of the stall.

Following her, he secured the latch. ''Funny how my reining operation couldn't support itself, yet it was Boyd who nearly *bankrupted* the entire ranch.''

Stunned by his words, she stopped in the middle of the corridor. Slowly, she turned to face him. ''How did you know about that?''

He approached her, looking sexy and too confident. A wild rebel. A dangerous renegade. A man who held her heart and didn't even know it. He stopped in front of her. To Brianne's immense relief he didn't touch her. He didn't have to. The heat emanating from him was stronger than a caress.

''Jasper told me,'' he finally answered her.

''I should have known,'' she said in disgust. Dragging her fingers through her hair, she turned and walked away. ''Jasper talks too much.''

Tyler grasped Brianne's arm, forcing her back around. ''You've done a great job with the ranch, Brianne. Jasper has a lot of respect for you. That's hard to come by.''

His touch singed her and brought on a rush of memories she didn't wanted to acknowledge. Memories of him holding her, kissing her, loving her... ''I couldn't have turned the ranch around without Jasper's support.''

His thumb caressed the sensitive skin just inside her

elbow, causing her pulse to career out of control. "I'm sorry you had to go through that all alone."

His sincerity was the last thing she wanted. "Well, ease your conscience, Tyler," she said, pulling her arm back from his grasp. "I came out of it just fine."

"That you did," he agreed, his voice dropping to a low, husky pitch. His heated gaze lowered to her mouth, and his head tilted to the side. "Are you sure you don't have a boyfriend I need to worry about?"

Frowning at him, she ignored the subtle pressure in her belly and the longing tugging at a forgotten place deep inside of her. "Why does it matter?"

Stepping toward her, he closed the distance between them and sifted both hands through her hair to cup the back of her head. His mouth curved in a devastatingly sexy smile. "Because I never make a move on a woman who's taken."

CHAPTER FIVE

STUNNED by Tyler's bold statement, Brianne gaped at him. Slow and easy, he maneuvered her three steps back, trapping her between the rough, wooden wall behind her and his strong, firm body. Her hands pressed against his muscled chest, but he didn't budge. The long, warm fingers tangled in her hair delved deeper, and his thumbs skimmed the line of her jaw, tipping her face up to his. Hot, hungry eyes fastened on her mouth.

Heat and tension vibrated between them. Against her will, she shivered. "Tyler, what are you doing?" Her whispered words were as shaky as she felt.

Something reckless and predatory lit his eyes. "I want you, Brianne."

She swallowed hard, wondering if this was a game to him, when she was so close to surrendering to the magic she knew they could create together. She would give him everything, heart and soul, and knew he'd scorn her when it was over.

"You don't want me," she said, finding her voice around the thickness of need gathering in her throat. "I'm just a convenient female body."

"No, I want *you,* Brianne." Lowering his head, he slid his lips over her jaw, to her ear. "I don't want to, but dammit, I do," he muttered.

Brianne groaned as his tongue touched the sensitive flesh just below her lobe. Her pulse raced and her fingers bit into his shoulders. Conflict raged within her. Her mind urged her to push him away while her heart fought to keep him near.

"We can't do this, Tyler," she said, even as her hands slid around his neck, her mouth turning toward the temptation of his. "We'll only end up hurting each other."

"Yeah, you're probably right," he agreed as he kissed the corner of her mouth then nipped at her bottom lip, drawing a gasp from her. "But it doesn't seem to make any difference. We both want each other too much."

Her lashes drifted close. "Tyler, please…"

"That sounds more like an invitation than a protest."

Confusion swirled around her like smoke. "No."

"Then tell me to stop and I will." His mouth opened against her neck, his breath fanning hot and damp across her skin. "Do it fast, Brianne, before I lose the control to stop."

Brianne ached for him, in an all-consuming way that kept her silent. For nine long years she'd stored her need and longing for him. Now, the outpouring of emotion overwhelmed her.

When his mouth claimed hers, she responded openly, holding nothing back. She didn't expect a tender, gentle kiss, and she didn't get one. Tyler's invasion was bold and greedy, the slide of his tongue against hers drugging and highly erotic. As if he couldn't get enough of her, he framed her face in his hands, angled her head, and slanted his mouth more fully over hers. He kissed her so deeply she trembled, until their mutual groans of pleasure and frustration mingled. Over and over he kissed her. Shamelessly. Desperately. Like a man gone too long from home.

The last emotion sent her over that fragile edge. She whimpered and clung to him. He tasted of the coffee and chocolate cake they'd had for dessert. Warm and silky. Like heaven. Like everything missing in her life. She gave him her heart and soul…and knew she'd offered herself to a man too embittered by the past to appreciate the gift he beheld.

Tears burned her eyes. Her kiss, her response, had everything to do with love; his had everything to do with a primitive need to possess. Possibly even meant to punish and hurt.

She turned her head away, breaking their heated kiss. "Don't." She struggled to move away, suddenly ashamed at her wild response. The flame between her and Tyler hadn't died over the years. It had merely been buried.

The thought was frightening.

He captured her chin and forced her to meet his gaze. "We weren't doing anything you didn't want to, Brianne."

No, she couldn't accuse him of taking advantage of her. But he played by different rules, rules that could break her heart and jeopardize her son's welfare.

She drew a deep breath, shoring her fortitude. "You're right, Tyler. I still want you, but I won't be one of your many conquests."

This time when she attempted to move away, he let her go.

Brianne itched to bake, but she'd used the last of the sugar in the morning's batch of confections. The next trip into town she planned to buy a twenty-five-pound sack.

She paced her bedroom, still shaken by the kiss she'd shared with Tyler. A hot, intense kiss that seared her soul and terrified her for all the suppressed emotions it unleashed. Hope. Longing. Need.

She swore she didn't need Tyler, and wouldn't make the mistake of depending on him again. For anything. The men in her life, from her own father, to Tyler, to

Boyd, had destroyed her trust at one time or another. She'd learned her lesson three times over. This time, she'd be nobody's fool, no matter how well that nobody kissed. Tyler represented heartache and broken promises, and she'd had too many of those in this lifetime.

And then there was the fanciful ideas he had for the ranch. She'd worked too hard rebuilding Whitmore Acres to risk a reining operation sure to eat up her profit and savings.

Brianne sat on the edge of the bed and buried her face in her hands, a frustrated moan escaping her. What was she going to do about Tyler's ambitious intentions?

For the next hour she agonized over her choices, discarding each one as she considered it. She paced, sat on her bed, and popped back up only to resume her agitated pattern across the bedroom floor. Since kicking Tyler off a ranch he half owned wasn't a viable choice, Brianne found her options very limited.

The only feasible solution, and least complicated one, was to purchase Tyler's share of the ranch. Tyler could take the cash, leave to pursue his aspirations of training and showing reining horses elsewhere, and she could continue in the peaceful existence her life had been before his arrival.

What if he didn't take the money, her conscience taunted as she went to her dresser and slipped on her nightgown. Refusing to consider the possibility, she shook the disturbing thought from her mind. He *had* to take the money.

With a sigh more weary than relieved, she turned down her bedcovers and crawled into bed. Despite her comforting decision to buy out Tyler, sleep eluded her. She tossed and turned, then stared at the shadows cast by the moonlight filtering into the room.

She thought of boiling the potatoes for tomorrow's

potato salad, but talked herself out of the chore. She didn't want to risk being alone with Tyler until she was ready to approach him with her business decision. And before she did that, she needed to review the books to see how much cash down payment she could come up with for the settlement.

And starting first thing tomorrow morning, that would be her goal.

How long did Brianne intend to avoid him?

Pondering that question, Tyler slapped together two peanut butter and jelly sandwiches for his lunch and poured himself a tall glass of cold milk.

His partner had made herself scarce the past couple of days, ever since the night he'd hinted at his intentions with the ranch...since the night he'd kissed her. Her avoidance both amused and irritated him.

Every morning she left breakfast warming in the oven for him, and disappeared into the office situated in the back of the indoor arena. Lunch, he was on his own. The three of them gathered at the dinner table in the evenings, but that didn't seem the appropriate time to further discuss his plans to start a reining operation. He fully expected another argument on the matter, and he refused to engage in a sparring match with Brianne in front of Daniel. He had a feeling she knew it, too, and used the boy's presence to her advantage.

Daniel. Tyler shook his head as he chewed a piece of sandwich and stared out the kitchen window. He was still trying to understand Brianne's son and the way he went out of his way to avoid him, too. Oftentimes he caught Daniel watching him in the breaking corral, his expression brooding, like he didn't trust him. Which was ludicrous. What had he done to earn such contempt from a nephew he'd never met before? The only thing he could figure was that Daniel was protecting his mother, or himself. But from what, Tyler couldn't fathom.

At any rate, he was determined to break through Daniel's reserve and prove he wasn't the threat Daniel might think he was.

As he chased down the last of his sandwich with the rest of his milk, he wondered what kind of relationship Daniel had with Boyd. Had they been close? As much as he tried, Tyler couldn't imagine Boyd suddenly possessing the patience and gentleness to deal with a toddler, and giving unselfishly of himself to spend quality, bonding time with a child.

With his hunger satisfied, Tyler left the kitchen and headed back to the breaking corral. He saw Daniel beneath a huge shade tree, pitching a baseball at a stretched piece of netting that bounced the ball back to him. His movements were lanky and awkward, his arms and legs not quite coordinating.

Remembering himself at Daniel's age and recognizing the determination etched on the boy's face, Tyler started in his direction. It seemed he and Daniel had something in common.

Daniel glanced over his shoulder as Tyler neared. Dismissing him without a word of acknowledgment, he threw the ball into the net. The ball rebounded, but Daniel missed the catch. The ball hit the tip of his glove and dropped to the ground, rolling to a stop by Tyler's booted foot.

Tyler picked up the baseball, watching the color rise in Daniel's face. "You play ball?"

"What does it look like I'm doing?" Daniel returned caustically, his back ramrod straight.

"Playing baseball?" Tyler guessed, injecting a light, humorous note to his voice.

Daniel's unfriendly expression didn't change. "Good guess," he said flatly. "Can I have it back?"

Tyler moved forward, but didn't return the ball. "Do you play on a league?"

Daniel's chin jutted out, his blue eyes darkening. "No. And I don't want to, either."

The defensive note in his voice put Tyler on alert. Remembering Boyd's taunts over his own inability to play baseball, he sought to put the boy at ease. "Yeah, it seems like a pretty silly game to me, too. All you do is throw a ball around and run in a big circle with someone chasing you."

Daniel didn't comment, just watched him warily.

Tyler rubbed his thumb over the course surface of the baseball. "I tried out for a league when I was about your age."

The tense set of Daniel's shoulders relaxed slightly, though his expression remained guarded. "Did you make it?"

"Yes, but only because they needed the players."

Daniel looked unconvinced. "What position did you play?"

"When I wasn't a bench warmer, I played right field." Which was the worst possible position available.

He gave a snort of doubt. "I don't believe you."

"It's true. Ask Jasper, he'll tell you the same thing. I couldn't play baseball worth a darn." Tyler glanced out into the pasture, watching the horses graze. "But there was one thing I could do exceptionally well."

"What?" The one word held hesitant interest.

Tyler met Daniel's gaze, knowing this was his one chance to reach the boy. "Ride horses. And train them. I've seen the way you handle Fiero and the rest of the horses. They respond well to you."

Daniel picked at a loose string on his leather glove. "I like working with the horses," he admitted quietly.

"And I think you'd make a fine trainer, but it takes a lot of hard work and dedication. I'd like you to think about my offer to teach you."

"Mom thinks I'm too young to learn how to break and train the horses." Apprehension edged out the hope lingering in his voice.

Tyler grinned. "Don't worry about your Mom. I can handle her." He glanced at his watch. "Tell you what. Jasper has a filly he wants me to break. Why don't you come and watch me, and if you decide you want to give it a try, this weekend we can start you on scheduled lessons."

Daniel's brows creased over his eyes. "You'd really want to teach me?"

"Only if you want to learn," Tyler replied, feeling a small sense of victory. "Think about it. I'll be over in the breaking corral if you want to watch."

Tyler tossed Daniel the ball and he caught it. The last thing Tyler saw before he turned away was the tentative smile on Daniel's face.

Heaving a frustrated sigh, Brianne tossed her pencil on the desk. She leaned back in her office chair, unable to concentrate on the figures in the financial journal spread open in front of her. The tiny office was suddenly suffocating.

Five days, and she still hadn't gotten used to Tyler being around, invading every portion of her life. He slept on the small, uncomfortable daybed without complaint. His male paraphernalia dominated the spare bathroom upstairs, and his earthy, masculine scent lingered long after he left the house each morning to work the horses with Jasper and Steven. If that wasn't enough for her to deal with, his gaze had an uncanny way of zeroing in on her when she entered the room.

It was driving her insane. *He* was driving her insane. And she had the suspicious feeling he knew it.

She made certain they were never alone. When Daniel went to bed, she retired, too, even though she rarely fell asleep until after eleven. She sat in bed reading a book, feeling like a prisoner in her own house, but unwilling to risk a confrontation with Tyler until it was on her terms.

Picking up her pencil, Brianne ignored the dull ache in her back from the hours spent sitting and bending over her desk. No matter how she scrimped and cut, she couldn't seem to pool enough cash to make the buyout worth Tyler's while. She racked her brain for hours, and days, and finally arrived at a feasible solution. She'd offer Tyler what cash she had available and either take a loan on the rest of the agreed amount, or make payments to him.

Satisfied with her plan, she did a budget of the next years' expenses, including feed, veterinary supplies, payroll, the mortgage, and other costs she incurred. She took into consideration the seventy-five acres she subleased to her neighbor for half of the alfalfa crop. No money crossed hands in that transaction, but the exchange covered a good portion of her feed bill for the winter.

She analyzed the balance in the account, deducted her budget, and came up with an immediate ten thousand dollars for Tyler. The cash expense would put her in a tight situation, but she'd worked with less and was confident she'd recoup the loss after six months.

She closed the ledger just as Jasper walked into the office, tracking in dust on her indoor/outdoor carpet from his boots. "Afternoon, boss," he greeted. Taking off his hat, he placed a yellow slip from the farrier in her "in" basket.

"Good afternoon, Jasper." Grabbing the invoice he'd deposited, she blanched at the amount. "When did Ellard raise his shoeing fee?"

"Last month." Jasper didn't look happy about the increase, either. "Said he sent out a notice."

"And I was conveniently left off his list," she muttered irritably, filing the invoice to pay next week. "Ellard is raising his fee every six months. It's getting ridiculous."

Jasper nodded, his fingers smoothing over the brim of the hat in his hands. "I think he sees how well the ranch is doin' and thinks you can afford the raise."

Brianne ground her teeth, knowing Jasper was right. Ellard was chauvinistic enough to take advantage of a woman, believing a mere female wouldn't question his motives for an increase. He was dead wrong.

"I won't be the one to support his alimony payments. Find another farrier, Jasper." She stood and stretched the kinks from her stiff body.

Jasper grinned, admiration sparkling in his eyes. "I'll get right on it, boss." He sauntered to the window facing the activity on the ranch. Steven's blond head passed by as he led a filly to the cutting paddock. "Have you decided which roofer you want to use to repair the leak in the stable yet?"

"I, uh, no," she replied, shuffling papers and files on her desk. In her scramble to buy Tyler's share of the ranch, she'd forgotten about the extra expense of repairing the stable roof. "It'll have to wait a few months."

Jasper glanced over his shoulder at her, a frown marring his bushy, gray brows. "A few months and it'll be rainy season. Best to get it repaired now, b'fore more damage is done."

"I know, Jasper," she said, inwardly cringing at the desperation lacing her voice. "But I don't have a choice right now." Pulling out a file containing a list of clients interested in purchasing a cutting horse, she made a mental note to call each to firm up a deal.

Jasper's gaze narrowed on her. She resisted the urge to squirm under his scrutiny. "What's goin' on, Miss Brianne? You in some kind of financial trouble?"

"Of course not." She dismissed his concern with a wave of her hand. She'd never lied to Jasper before, and she hated doing so now. But she refused to tell him her plans, knowing the old man would try and talk her out of her decision. Despite Tyler's past indiscretions, she knew Jasper was very fond of him. "Things are just going to be tight for the next few months. Before I spend a big chunk of money, I want to be certain we can afford to do so."

He didn't believe her. She could see it in the grim line of his mouth and his ridged stance. He rested his arm on top of the metal file cabinet next to the window. "How long you gonna avoid him?"

Uncomfortable with Jasper's prying, Brianne turned and shoved the financial journal back into the huge metal safe behind her desk. "Who am I avoiding?" she asked breezily, facing Jasper again.

He lifted a brow. "Tyler, that's who."

Her chin lifted a fraction. "I'm not avoiding him."

"Sure you are," he replied relentlessly.

"That's absurd." Crossing her arms over her chest, she gave him a tolerant look. "I can hardly avoid Tyler when we're living under the same roof."

The corner of his mouth curled into a slight smile. "Funny, I hear from Tyler you've been slippin' off to bed when Daniel does. He laughed and said you must be one of those females who needs your beauty rest, but he's not stupid, Miss Brianne."

Her beauty rest! She blew out an upstream breath that ruffled her bangs. "It's been an exhausting week."

"I'm sure it gets real exhausting bein' holed up in this little ol' office," he mocked.

"I've been working," she defended, stepping around the desk and coming toward him. "I had inventory to take care of, the books to go over, payroll to do, and I sold Gentleman Dan and Elijah Blue." She ticked each chore off on her fingers.

Jasper looked unimpressed. "I sold the geldings, you wrote up the paperwork and accepted the check." His gaze softened. "You've never spent this much time in the office."

She glanced away, focusing on a picture of a prized cutting horse from Landon's day. "Well, maybe it's time I did." At least until Tyler was gone.

"You haven't ridden Cameo in four days."

She jammed her flattened hands into the back pockets of her faded jeans. "Put her on the hot walker to stretch her legs."

His lips pursed. "You never put her on the hot walker, and you ride her at least every other day. Or you had until Tyler arrived."

Brianne winced at the accusation and turned away. Absently, she straightened the manuals on horse breeds lining the bookshelf beside her.

"If you're not locked in the office, you're up at the house bakin'," Jasper went on. "I don't mind the goodies, mind you, but Betty is startin' to complain that I'm gonna end up with a potbelly if you don't quit with the sweets."

Brianne heard the humor in his voice, and the genuine concern. She wanted to tell him to stop worrying, that she'd be fine once Tyler was gone. A blatant lie, considering she'd have an aching heart to contend with. Again.

It was past time to switch gears on their verbal exchange. "How are you coming on that filly you're training for the Circle M?"

He stared at her for a long moment before answering. "Jus' fine. Another week and she'll be ready to go."

"Good." She forced a bright smile. "Larry mentioned he might be interested in a few more cutters. I'll contact him and see what he's decided."

"What's the big rush?"

She slanted him a look. "We could use the money to repair the stable roof."

"You had the money b'fore Larry contacted us. What happened?"

She didn't want to tell Jasper it was none of his business what happened to the money, because he'd made Whitmore Acres his business for longer than she'd been alive. He'd stuck with her through the good and bad times. He didn't deserve to be hurt that way. "Jasper, please, just trust me. We're going to need the money."

"What're you plannin' on doin'?" His age-old eyes bore into hers. "Buy Tyler out?"

Brianne's stomach dropped. She broke their stare, not wanting to see the condemnation sure to flare in his eyes when she confirmed his question. "It's for the best, Jasper."

"Best for whom?" Jasper's tone was controlled and even, but an unmistakable thread of anger ran through the words. She opened her mouth to reply, but he cut her off. "He's a good man, missy. He's made a few mistakes in the past, but haven't we all?"

Brianne's shoulders slumped in defeat. How could she justify her purpose to Jasper, to make him understand she was trying to ensure her and Daniel's future? She was going to have a hard enough time rationalizing her reasons to Tyler. It was either pay now financially, or suffer later emotionally.

"You don't understand—"

"I understand he's an asset to the ranch. He's a hard worker. He ain't afraid to get a little sh...dirt on his boots, and he's got a deft touch with the horses." He looked out the window, a slow smile spreading across his face. "Well I'll be damned. It looks like Tyler even has Daniel's attention."

And Jasper had Brianne's attention. She was on the verge of making a cash deal with Tyler to leave; she couldn't afford to let Daniel get emotionally attached to him.

Grabbing her hat off the wooden rack by the door, she jammed it purposefully on her head. "I think I'll take Cameo out for a run. And maybe I'll ask Tyler to join me." She gave Jasper a placating smile, even as her mind reviewed her strategy for approaching Tyler with her bargain.

"Good idea," Jasper said, satisfaction in his voice.

Striding past him, she stepped outside. The day was summertime hot, but the warm rays did nothing to penetrate the deep chill within her. For all her bravado with Jasper, Brianne wished she maintained more confidence that Tyler was going to accept her offer.

Shoring her determination, she headed toward the paddock where Tyler was blanket-breaking a particularly skittish two-year-old filly, convincing herself Tyler's departure would hurt all of them less now, than later. And his leaving was inevitable, a dark, depressing cloud that would hang over her until Tyler decided he'd had enough of her cozy family life and returned to the show circuit he'd favored the past couple of years.

Daniel stood at the fencing near where Tyler worked the horse. Brianne slowly approached her son. Arms braced on the second rung of the railing, his intense expression indicated his absorption in the easy way Tyler handled the spirited filly.

Indeed, Brianne found herself captivated by Tyler's silky, cajoling voice. His back was to them as he walked the chestnut. A chocolate brown Stetson on his head shielded his eyes from the sun. He held on to the halter with one hand, while the other gently swept a blanket on the horse's back. The filly sidestepped away, dancing anxiously, unused to the sensation of weight on its back.

"It's okay, girl," Tyler soothed in a low, comforting tone. Stroking the filly's glistening neck, he calmed the animal with his touch and voice. "That's not so bad, now is it? What a pretty girl you are."

Such tenderness, Brianne thought with a pang of longing she immediately dismissed. She didn't want Tyler's tenderness, she told herself, and almost believed the lie. Right now, she wanted his cooperation.

She stepped beside Daniel. "How ya doin', kiddo?" she asked in a low voice so as not to disturb Tyler's training.

A startled look passed over Daniel's features, as if she'd shaken him out of a trance. The avid sparkle in his eyes faded and his face flushed. Brianne realized she'd embarrassed him by catching him so fascinated with Tyler.

"Okay, I guess," he muttered, his expression once again guarded.

She ran her fingers though his sun-warmed hair. A well of regret rushed through her, that he'd missed the close bond shared by most fathers and sons. And now, she was going to steal his only chance to know his true father.

Closing her eyes against the multitude of doubts crowding her heart, she firmly told herself she was doing the right thing. The lecture seemed harder to swallow this time.

"What do you think, Daniel?" Tyler asked. Removing the blanket from the horse, he glanced their way. His gaze landed on Brianne, registering mild surprise before continuing on to Daniel. "You've been watching me work with this filly for the past hour. Would you like to give her a try?"

Brianne watched her son wage a silent war with himself, struggling with the desire to accept the challenge of handling the horse, and fighting the distrust that automatically reared when a male figure offered something so tempting. Acceptance flitted over his features, and Brianne knew, and suddenly feared, that Daniel was about to impart his first branch of trust.

"Tyler, can I talk with you?" Brianne blurted.

Tyler's gaze melded with hers, and a muscle in his jaw ticked. Her heart leaped into her throat, knowing he knew she'd deliberately sabotaged his attempt to interact with Daniel.

Looking away, Tyler led the filly to an awning providing water and shade for the horse. "Would you mind taking over here, Daniel, and put Banshee away?" he drawled easily to the boy. "Looks like I've been summoned by the boss."

Hesitantly, Daniel moved forward. Meeting Tyler under the awning, he shyly took Banshee's lead rope. Tyler murmured something to Daniel Brianne couldn't hear, and Daniel nodded. Tyler squeezed his shoulder, and Daniel led the filly toward the stable. The bright, eager light in his eyes boosted Brianne's diligence to cut all ties with Tyler.

Tyler walked out of the paddock and toward her. A

blue T-shirt defined his muscular chest, and soft, worn jeans clung intimately to his body. With every step, his boots kicked up a swirl of dust. His hat cast shadows over his features, giving him a dark and dangerous appeal. She checked the impulse to take a huge step back for every one that drew him near.

Stopping inches from her, he tipped his hat back, a glimmer of mockery in his eyes. "To what do I owe this pleasure?"

A batch of butterflies fluttered wildly in her stomach, from nerves, and his nearness. Heat emanated off him, and it had nothing to do with the sun. The pull was there, a dangerous attraction threatening to sweep her away.

She rubbed her damp palms down her denim clad thighs. "I, um, was wondering if we could take the horses out for a ride?"

Tyler stared at Brianne. Something was up. Her anxiety was tangible, radiating off her stronger than electricity. "Why do I get the feeling this isn't a pleasure outing?"

"It's strictly business, Tyler," she said firmly.

He shrugged lazily, though he burned with curiosity. "Fine. I need to saddle up Sweet Justice."

She gave him a curt nod and spun around, walking toward the stable housing her mare, Cameo.

Tyler stood there, watching her longer and more boldly than what was appropriate. Her back was ramrod straight, but he knew with the right amount of stroking she'd soften and purr like a kitten, just as she had the night he'd kissed her. His blood stirred at the memory, kicking off a chain reaction of need and longing that tapped a secluded, remote part of him. Ruthlessly, he shoved the emotions aside, refusing to give in to feelings he had no use for.

The lady wanted to talk business. So did he. He had a ranch to reclaim, and a champion reining horse to purchase.

CHAPTER SIX

TYLER wondered when she'd get around to speaking. They were a half mile from the house in the east pasture, their horses strolling at a lazy pace. The creak of leather and a soft snort from the mares were the only sounds adding to the tranquillity of the afternoon ride.

She finally looked at him, shoulders back, head high. "I want to buy your half of the ranch," she announced solemnly.

Tyler couldn't have been more stunned if she'd told him she was from another planet. He thought he'd made it clear he had no intention of going anywhere. But she'd either misunderstood or hadn't been listening.

He laughed, but the sound lacked humor. "You'd like that, wouldn't you, Bree? And the first thing you'd probably do is kick me off the property."

Irritation shot gold through the amber hue of her eyes. "I'll make it worth your while."

"Really?" He slid his gaze over her, taking in her beautiful face and soft, kissable mouth. He wondered if she thought a night in his bed would be worth his while. Would she sell herself to claim the entire Whitmore estate? She'd sold out to Boyd... His jaw clenched at the recollection, and the hurt and betrayal accompanying the memory.

"What would you give to see me gone?" he asked, his voice rough with resentment.

She glanced at him, all prim and business-like. "I've come up with ten thousand cash to give you—"

"No way."

81

"And I'll make additional payments until I've paid you your fair share. That's the best I can do."

Her determination to be rid of him sparked the fury simmering just below the surface. "You just don't get it, do you? Well let me explain it one more time. I'm content here. I've signed the papers for the ranch, and I'm not about to give you the satisfaction of getting rid of me. In fact," he added, his tone rising to an angry pitch that caused Sweet Justice to prance nervously, "you can count me as a permanent roommate. I'm not giving up the land, and I'm not moving out of the house."

Her face paled. "You can't be serious!"

"I'm very serious," he said with quiet finality. He stared off into the distance, then said, "I want to purchase a reining stud."

Brianne breathed deeply, attempting to tamp the panic squeezing her chest. Her proposition had backfired, and now Tyler was steamrollering ahead with his reckless plans. "The ranch can't afford that kind of risk."

"The ranch can't afford a stud, yet you were going to spend nearly every spare cent you had to get rid of me?" His tone held mild reproach.

Guilt assailed her, but she shoved it aside. "That's different."

"Yeah, I suppose it is." His shrewd gaze held hers. "Giving *me* the cash wouldn't be a risk, but an investment, right?"

An *emotional* investment, yes, she wanted to tell him, but the words caught in her throat and ripped at her heart.

"If you're so hot to invest your money, invest it wisely," he continued, talking as if they'd been running the ranch and making business decisions together for years. "I want to purchase Roman Warrior, the reining stud I told you about."

Tyler was moving too fast, invading her territory and turning her life upside down. She had no idea how to thwart his plans except to refuse what he wanted.

"No," she finally said, coolly meeting his gaze.

"No?" A cynical smile curled the corners of his mouth. "In case this minor fact has slipped your mind, half this ranch is mine. I'll find a way to purchase Roman Warrior with or without your permission."

Her temper shot to the boiling point, but she held her anger in check. Why had she believed his leaving would be as simple as handing him some cash and waving as he drove out of town?

"How much is this stud you want so badly?" she asked calmly, disguising the deeper layer of anxiety coiling in her.

"Armon Eckerly, my former employer, is asking forty thousand."

"Forty thousand!" She gaped at him, reeling at the staggering amount he mentioned so casually.

"I could probably get him down to thirty grand and limited breeding rights. He owes me a few favors."

Her fingers curled around the pommel in a white-knuckle grip. "That would totally deplete my reserves! I can't do it."

"We *can* do it," he insisted. "I have about twelve grand saved from the competitions I've won—"

"Which leaves us eight thousand short."

"We can take a short-term loan with the bank."

She scoffed at that. "Considering the phenomenal success of the last reining operation I'm sure they'll laugh us out of the bank."

Something dark and bitter brewed in his gaze, but he didn't argue her point. "We can sell a few acres."

"No," she said adamantly. "I didn't save this ranch to turn around and sell chunks of it. Whitmore Acres is all Daniel has. I won't risk any of it for something as chancy as your reining operation!"

"You're being unreasonable," he said in a low, heated tone.

"*I'm* being unreasonable?" she asked, shooting him an incredulous look. "I'm not the one who walked away from the ranch nine years ago! You didn't care what happened to me, your father, or the ranch. I've worked hard to keep Whitmore Acres from going into bankruptcy. The cutting operation is finally profitable and respected. I won't let you and your wild ideas of another reining operation destroy the ranch's reputation."

Tyler's body tensed. "The reining operation *never* jeopardized Whitmore Acre's reputation. Boyd sabotaged my business *and* nearly bankrupted the ranch."

Tyler's claim momentarily shocked her. She hadn't been blind to Boyd's cunning and greed, but what Tyler suggested was outrageous. Or was it?

Not wanting to ponder the possibility, she focused on her main goal. "I don't want you here, Tyler," she said firmly. "If you were smart, you'd take my offer and put a down payment on a place of your own."

"I already have a place of my own."

Knowing she was losing the battle of wills, she spurred Cameo into a run. The landscape passed in a blur. Leaning low over the animal's neck, Brianne urged the mare faster and faster, as if she could escape the devil behind her.

The devil was right on her heels, then beside her. A thunderous expression lined Tyler's features, and his eyes blazed with anger. Sweet Justice effortlessly matched Cameo's pace over the rolling, green pasture.

"Goddammit, Brianne, slow down before you break your neck!"

Ignoring his warning, she pushed Cameo harder. Sweet Justice's speed accelerated, too. Adrenaline pumped through Brianne's blood as Tyler maneuvered his horse dangerously close to hers.

Reaching out, he grabbed her reins and slowly pulled them back. As furious as she was with Tyler for the foolish act, she knew better than to fight him and possibly harm Cameo.

He skillfully brought the horses to a halt. As soon as it was safe, Brianne slid off her mare and sprinted away. She didn't care where she headed as long as it was away from Tyler.

"Dammit, Brianne!" Tyler shouted. Dismounting Sweet Justice, he dropped both horses's reins so they could graze. "Get the hell back here. I'm not done talking to you!"

"Just leave me alone!" She stumbled over an uneven patch of grass, caught herself, and kept trudging forward. The sun beat down on her, dampening her brow with perspiration.

Tyler's colorful curse broke the quiet. His booted steps sounded behind her, until he was at her side, matching her stride. "I'm not leaving you alone until we settle this." His tone was uncompromising.

She glared at him. "There's nothing to settle. Half of Whitmore Acres belongs to *me*, and I refuse to support your reining operation." Her words were harsh, prompted by a fear she couldn't control. "Unless you can come up with a quick eight grand in cash, we're at a stalemate."

Tyler's furious expression remained embedded in Brianne's mind for the rest of the afternoon. He'd looked as though he'd wanted to strangle her, but protecting her livelihood had been her primary concern. She wasn't about to assist Tyler with his destructive plans. At least not without a fight.

He didn't come up to the house for dinner that evening. Brianne was relieved; she didn't want to pretend being amiable in front of Daniel.

By ten o'clock that same evening Tyler still hadn't made an appearance. Turning off the lights in the house except for the porch light, she went upstairs. From her bedroom she could see the stables. A light illuminated the interior. Standing at the window, she wondered what consumed Tyler's attention for so many hours.

Convincing herself she didn't care, she changed into her nightgown and crawled into bed, but sleep eluded her. She stayed awake, waiting until she heard Tyler come into the house before she allowed herself to succumb to sleep.

She woke the following morning, feeling surprisingly refreshed and able to analyze her dilemma with Tyler from a clearer perspective. If he was determined to stay, she had no legal recourse. In order to work together on a daily basis, they had to reach a compromise.

She hadn't changed her mind about his reining operation, but she hoped he'd be open to helping Jasper with the cutting business until they resolved, or dissolved, their partnership. It was the best solution she could come up with.

Dressed and ready for the day ahead, Brianne went downstairs to start breakfast. Tyler wasn't in the house. Glancing out the kitchen window, she noticed his truck and trailer were gone.

A strong sense of intuition wove through her, sweeping her back in time. Before she even looked, she knew she wouldn't find Tyler's duffel bag in the guest room.

A glance in the upstairs bathroom showed it free of his male paraphernalia. She searched for a note, but didn't find one.

Despising the sharp jab of dread near the vicinity of her heart, she went to the stables, needing one last piece of evidence to confirm her suspicion.

Sweet Justice's empty stall was all the proof she needed.

Resting her forehead on the stall's gate, she squeezed her eyes closed. "Damn him," she said, her voice choked with a multitude of emotions. How could he do this to her, again?

"Something wrong, Miss Brianne?"

Brianne spun around at the sound of Jasper's concerned tone. He stood in the corridor, a currycomb in hand.

"Where's Tyler?" Surely he'd told *someone* where he was going.

"I don't know," Jasper replied with a shrug. "He didn't say anything to me about leavin', but I did hear him pull out 'bout four this mornin'."

She shook her head, a brittle laugh escaping her. "This is just like Tyler, to run at the first sign of trouble."

Jasper's gaze held sympathy. "Be careful what you wish for, missy."

His words stung, making *her* feel like the villain. Yes, she'd wanted Tyler to leave. Except she hated the way he'd orchestrated his departure. "He didn't even have the courtesy to say goodbye or tell me where he's heading."

Jasper placed the currycomb on a nearby shelf. "What makes you think he's gone for good?"

"He took Sweet Justice," she said, angrily waving a

hand toward the empty stall. "He didn't leave anything behind."

Jasper nodded in understanding. "So, he accepted your offer to buy him out?"

"No. He refused the money." She paced the area, kicking up straw with every step. "He wanted to start another reining operation, and I told him I wouldn't support it. Not after what happened the last time, and especially not when Whitmore Acres is finally turning a decent profit."

Jasper propped a booted foot on a bench running the length of the corridor. "A reining operation wouldn't be such a bad thing."

She stopped abruptly, unable to believe what she was hearing. "How can you say that after the disastrous outcome of the last reining operation?"

"Tyler's got another nine years' reining experience on him. Breeding, training *and* showing. I'm sure he's learned enough 'bout the business to run the operation efficiently."

She released a frustrated stream of breath. "I don't know why I'm arguing about this when he's not coming back."

A small smile played around Jasper's mouth. "I wouldn't be too sure 'bout that, missy."

She rolled her eyes at Jasper's confidence in Tyler. She'd had personal experience with his desertion and knew better than to count on him returning anytime soon. She'd no doubt bruised his pride by denying him the reining operation.

The one thing that nagged at her is that he hadn't taken the money she'd offered. Had he been angry enough to walk away from everything without any compensation?

She spent the day in her office pondering that question, wishing she knew the answer. Everything would be okay, she reassured herself. Believing the lecture came easily until Daniel approached her that night while she was preparing dinner.

"Where did Uncle Tyler go, Mom?" he asked tentatively, watching as she filled a stockpot with water for spaghetti. "He's been gone all day."

Brianne's heart jumped into her throat. She knew Daniel would ask about Tyler, but she wasn't prepared to deal with the fallout of his sudden exit from their lives. She silently cursed him for putting her in this heart-wrenching predicament.

Carrying the pot to the stove, she put it on the back burner, then gave Daniel her full attention. She smoothed her hand over his silky hair in a comforting gesture. "I'm not sure where he went, honey."

A frown creased his brows. "Will he be back this weekend?"

She thought about lying, but knew she couldn't give him false hopes. Judging by past actions, the chances of Tyler returning were slim. "I don't think so."

He stared at his sneakers, shoulders hunched. "I knew it," he muttered beneath his breath.

"Daniel, what's up?" she asked, unable to shake that awful sense of unease within her.

He backed away from her, raising that invisible wall of defense over his true emotions. "He promised to start teaching me to break the fillies this weekend. I should have known he wouldn't be around."

The very life of her deflated. Her son's self-esteem was fragile enough without Tyler contributing to the problem. "Oh, Daniel, I'm so sorry."

His chin lifted, but his bottom lip trembled slightly. "It doesn't matter. I didn't want to do it anyhow." He whirled around and ran upstairs to his room. The slamming of the door reverberated through the house and Brianne's heart.

Brianne wanted to call Daniel back, but nothing she could say or do would make the situation any better. His hopes had been crushed. She'd tried protecting him from this kind of hurt, but nothing would have prepared Daniel for the truth. For the second time in his young life, the man who'd fathered him had walked away without a backward glance.

The long weekend passed without any word from Tyler. Daniel moped the entire time, unable to understand why his uncle Tyler had left without saying goodbye. He'd even asked if he'd done something wrong to make Tyler leave. Resenting Tyler's irresponsible treatment, the tension within Brianne built. She'd wanted him off the ranch, but not at the expense of her son's emotions.

Sighing wearily, Brianne pushed thoughts of Tyler aside. She had a business to run. Staring at the feed invoice in her hand, she tried concentrating on her Monday afternoon task of paying bills and balancing the books. She ran a tape on the invoice's figures and came up with three different totals. Frustrated with her inability to focus on work, she set the slip of paper aside and rubbed her throbbing temples.

The rattling sound of a truck and trailer pulling into the drive caught her attention. Not expecting any deliveries or pickups, her chest tightened with apprehension. Had Tyler returned?

Standing, she skirted her desk and stepped outside, confirming her suspicions. Tyler stood by his trailer talking to Jasper, smiling and joking with the older man as if he didn't have a care in the world. As if he hadn't been absent for four days...as if he hadn't broken promises to the young boy slinking off to the main house.

A slow burning fury churned in her as she marched purposefully in Tyler's direction. Nearing the duo, she heard Tyler mention the exposition he'd attended over the weekend, which explained where he'd disappeared to, but in no way excused the manner in which he'd left.

Tyler glanced her way, his smile slowly fading. "Hello, Brianne," he said pleasantly.

She barely managed to restrain her temper. "Tyler." Her acknowledgment was curt. "Can I see you in my office?"

He walked to the tailgate of the trailer and unlatched the lock. "Sure, just as soon as I unload Sweet Justice—"

"I'd like to talk to you *now*." She wasn't waiting another minute. Before he could argue, or she exploded in front of everyone, she turned and walked back toward the indoor arena.

Tyler stared after Brianne, the elation of the past twenty-four hours fizzling. "What's her problem?" he asked Jasper.

Jasper took off his hat and scratched his head. "I reckon she was worried about you."

"Sure," Tyler replied wryly as he dropped the trailer ramp. "Worried that I'd come back."

Jasper chuckled. "I'm sure that's part it. You go on. I'll take care of Sweet Justice."

"Thanks." Taking off his Stetson and tossing it in the cab of his truck, he headed toward the ranch's office at a clipped pace.

He wasn't in the mood to deal with Brianne's attitude problem. All he'd thought about on the long drive home from Eugene, Oregon, was a long, hot shower and a home-cooked meal. He had a feeling neither would be his anytime soon.

After their heated argument, he'd deliberately given

her the weekend alone to calm down. He'd seen the reining exposition as the perfect opportunity to give Brianne some space, and for him to possibly gain the extra cash he needed to purchase Roman Warrior. Luck had been on his side, and he'd won the annual reining competition.

As soon as he stepped into the cool interior of Brianne's office she turned from her position at the window, her face flushed with anger. "What the hell do you think you're doing?" she asked in a blistering tone.

He closed the door, determined not to be baited into a fight. "Well, I was just about to unload Sweet Justice—"

"Don't be a smart-ass, Tyler," she said scathingly, her eyes the color of hot molten gold. "You've been gone four days without so much as a word, and then you waltz back as if you've never left. You can't just come and go as you please."

He crossed his arms over his chest, his patience thinning. "You're right. Someone might get the idea that I own half the place."

"Damn you!" She circled to stand behind her desk. "Even if you were angry with me you could have told Jasper you were leaving!"

He'd been on his own for so long, he'd forgotten what it was like to check in with someone. "I didn't think I needed to account for my whereabouts."

"It's called courtesy, Tyler, something you seem to lack."

"I didn't realize you cared," he shot back.

Bracing her hands flat on the desk, she leaned toward him, eyes narrowed. "I, personally, don't give a damn what you do. You can go to *hell* for all I care. But I won't let you put Daniel's emotions through the wringer just because you decide on a whim to take off for a competition and not tell anyone. You promised Daniel you'd start him on lessons this weekend.''

He swore beneath his breath. He'd been so angered by their argument and driven to win the purse that he hadn't given any thought beyond his own problems.

None of that was any excuse for hurting the boy.

Propping his arm on the wall, he stared out the window. He'd seen Daniel as he'd pulled up and now understood why the boy had gone up to the house instead of greeting him.

Damn. He had some explaining to do.

"You gave him nothing but broken promises, Tyler," she accused, her voice catching on emotion.

He glanced over his shoulder, seeing the condemnation in her expression...and hurt, too. "I didn't think about that," he said, genuinely apologetic for his negligence.

She scowled at him. "That's the problem, Tyler. You didn't think of anyone but yourself. What you did was irresponsible and hurtful, and I won't tolerate it.''

He turned and walked toward the desk separating them. "I don't know why you thought I wasn't coming back," he said with the slightest edge. "I've told you I'm not leaving the ranch.''

A bitter smile touched her mouth. "You don't have a great track record for sticking around, Tyler. What was I supposed to think?''

As if she'd slapped him with her words, he finally understood the root of her fury. She was remembering the first time he'd left after being denied his dreams...and hadn't returned for nine years. He'd hurt her back then, but she'd inflicted her own pain on him, too, when she'd married Boyd.

Still, he knew she had the right to be upset with him.

And if they were going to be partners, they had to put the past aside so they could move forward.

He started around the desk. "Brianne, I never meant to—"

"Don't," she cut him off, rounding the opposite side of the desk. "I don't want to hear any excuses." She opened the office door, but stopped before stepping through the threshold. "You've got some apologizing to do. I suggest you start with Daniel."

Tyler stared at the sign on Daniel's closed bedroom door, Enter At Your Own Risk, and wondered if he dared trespass any further. He'd never been any good at apologizing, but beyond this door was a boy who'd had his hopes dashed. He debated whether or not to wait until Daniel came out of hiding, but Daniel's anger wasn't something he wanted to let fester.

He raised his fist and knocked.

"Yeah," came the hostile reply.

He rubbed the belt buckle in his hand, as if the polished gold would lend him support. "It's your uncle Tyler. Can I come in?"

No answer.

Tyler tried the knob and found it unlocked. Opening the door, he peered inside the room. Daniel sat on a window seat, legs drawn up and arms wrapped around his knees. He continued staring out the window, even though Tyler knew he'd heard him enter.

Daniel had reverted to the same unapproachable kid he'd been when Tyler had first met him. Because of a wild impulse, all the headway he'd made with Daniel his first week on the ranch had been demolished.

Brianne was right. He'd thought of no one but himself. The realization was tough to swallow.

"Daniel," he began, crossing the room cluttered with clothes and toys. "I'm sorry about this weekend."

Daniel turned his head, looking at him with hauntingly familiar blue eyes. "It's okay. I'm used to it. Boyd...my *dad* always made promises he didn't keep."

His words cut deep. Tyler didn't especially like being compared to his half-brother. "I should have told you I was leaving for a few days, but I wasn't exactly thinking straight when I left." The excuse, as honest as it was, sounded lame even to his own ears. "It won't happen again."

"Sure." Daniel glanced back out the window again, silently dismissing him.

This was going to be tougher than he'd thought. Sitting on the edge of the bed across from Daniel, he attempted to explain his reasons for his absence. "What I did, my leaving for the weekend, was very important. There's a horse I want to buy, and I was hoping to win the extra money I needed at a reining expo in Eugene. I disappointed you," he admitted. "I'm hoping you can give me another chance, Daniel."

"Why should I?" he asked coolly.

Tyler braced his elbows on his spread knees. He turned the belt buckle over in his hands, thinking how something so valuable had cost him so much. "Because people make mistakes they regret. *I* made a mistake I regret."

Daniel was quiet for so long, Tyler finally stood, knowing there wasn't anything else he could do to make the boy forgive him. Maybe Daniel just needed time to digest their conversation. With a defeated sigh, he started for the door.

"Did you win?"

The abrupt question took Tyler by surprise. Stopping in the middle of Daniel's room, he turned. Daniel watched him speculatively, a subdued glimmer of interest in his gaze. Tyler pounced on it. "Yeah, I won the purse. And when they gave me this belt buckle, the first thing I thought of was giving it to you."

"To me?" His brows creased suspiciously. "Why?"

"Because I wanted you to have it, so whenever you look at it you'll remember that you can do anything you set your mind to."

He snorted. "I can't play baseball."

Tyler smiled at his skepticism. "Ah, but maybe you don't really want to."

"I'd rather work the horses," he admitted, ducking his head sheepishly.

"Then follow your dreams." Tyler returned to Daniel. Pressing the heavy gold into the boy's palm, he folded his small fingers over it. "*Anything* is possible."

Daniel opened his hand and stared at Tyler's trophy in awe. "Wow," he breathed, eyes wide. "Can I really keep this?"

Tyler nodded. "On one condition."

Daniel traced the deep imprint of a cowboy on a bucking horse, then looked at Tyler. "What's that?"

"You give me another chance."

A slow grin blossomed on Daniel's face. "Deal."

CHAPTER SEVEN

TYLER wished Brianne was as easy to sway as her son.

She had avoiding him down to a science. For three days she walked out of rooms he entered, ignored him when he commented on something, and avoided being completely alone with him. She went to her room after dinner. In the morning she left breakfast warming in the oven and retreated to her office.

He needed to talk with her, and suspected she knew the reason, thus her evasion. Ten thousand dollars cash in winnings was burning a hole in his pocket, and Roman Warrior wasn't getting any younger.

By Thursday, Tyler figured he'd given Brianne enough time to cool her temper. He entered the stables, where he'd last seen her disappear to, and spotted her in one of the stalls.

He'd never thought of mucking out stalls as arousing, but Brianne gave the task a whole new perspective. She was bent slightly as she raked up debris. Faded jeans, frayed at the curve of her bottom, outlined trim hips and long, slender legs. She'd tied her blouse just below her breasts, giving him a glimpse of silky-looking flesh.

Awareness hummed through him, heating his blood. The sensation wasn't at all unpleasant.

He leaned against the open gate. Slipping his fingers into the front pockets of his jeans, he touched the tissue wrapping a gift he'd bought for her at the exposition. A peace offering, he hoped.

He cleared his throat. "Brianne, can I talk to you?"

She tensed for a second, then continued her chore with renewed vigor. "I'm busy."

He suspected she'd be "busy" for the rest of her life when it came to him. "That's okay. I'll talk, you work."

She stopped her raking and faced him. Annoyance darted from her gaze. "What do you want, Tyler?"

At the moment, he could think of a hundred things he wanted from her, none of which applied to the business he needed to address. Withdrawing the small token from his pocket, he extended it toward her. "This is for you."

She stared at the tissue-wrapped package suspiciously. "I don't want anything from you."

Except to see him gone for good, he thought. "Quit being so stubborn and take the damn thing!"

Propping the rake against the wall, she tentatively took the parcel from his hand. Frowning, she peeled the tissue away with her gloved fingers slowly, as if he'd given her a bomb. Reaching the core of wrapping, she revealed an ornate silver and turquoise hairclip.

She glanced up at him. Her eyes lit with pleasure, before more cautious emotions took over. "What's this for?"

"A bribe?" He grinned recklessly.

Her mouth tightened, dispelling any softness of moments ago. "And now I'm supposed to forget everything that happened?"

"Something like that," he admitted. "I left angry, but I had a lot of time to think while I was in Eugene. You backed me in a corner and left me few choices. I *had* to enter that reining competition."

"You still should have told me where you were going."

"You're right, but I didn't, and now I've paid the consequences. I'm tired of arguing and fighting, Brianne."

She turned away without agreeing and placed the hair-clip on a nearby shelf. Swiping the back of her hand across the perspiration dotting her forehead, she grabbed the rake. "I need to get back to work," she said quietly.

He shoved his fingers through his hair in frustration. Unwilling to be dismissed so easily, he said, "I won the purse."

"Good for you," she replied blandly.

"It was ten grand."

She roughly scraped up a pile of hay and horse droppings. "Congratulations."

"I won it for *us*."

Brianne drew a deep breath of pungent smells, trying to keep her distress from surfacing. She knew what Tyler was hinting, but her feelings about a reining operation hadn't changed. "I don't want any part of your money."

"It's operating capital," Tyler persisted. "Now we can afford to purchase Roman Warrior."

The stable walls closed around her, until she thought she'd suffocate. Tossing the rake aside, she squeezed past Tyler into the corridor. Before she could escape him, he snagged her arm and whirled her around. The heat of his fingers sent spears of electricity racing up her arm.

Impatience etched his features. "What are you so afraid of?"

You. Us. My future. But she didn't say any of those things, knowing he would never understand. How could he, when he was the source of all her fears?

"I'm offering you a proposition that has the potential to make us good money," he said, releasing her arm. "You could be making money hand over fist."

She laughed, the sound catching in her dry throat. "Just like it did nine years ago?"

His jaw tightened. "The reining operation didn't fail, Boyd sucked it dry."

She stared at him incredulously. "What?"

"I'm sure you heard a much different story," he said, his tone defensive and bitter. "Probably the same lie Boyd told Landon that made him shut down the operation."

Brianne's first reaction was disbelief, but she knew what devious ploys Boyd was capable of. She'd also witnessed his impulsive spending habits that had taken the entire ranch to the brink of bankruptcy.

Digesting that thought, she pulled off her gloves and set them aside. "Is there any proof that Boyd skimmed?"

Tyler shrugged. "I doubt it."

"Surely Landon's accountants would have discovered some kind of evidence while reviewing the books."

"Not necessarily. A person can embezzle for years and never get caught." His gaze softened. "Brianne, I need you to trust me on this, and have faith in my ability to run a profitable reining operation."

Everything within her wanted to rebel. Trusting him meant heartache. "Tyler, please. We can't do this. The cost, the risk—"

"We'll recoup the cost in stud services alone in a few years," he argued. "Roman's a healthy, powerful Quarter horse with excellent bloodlines. We'll breed Sweet Justice for a sure winner for competing, and you've got a good stock of brood mares we can breed him to. We can build a solid base of reining and pleasure horses to sell. And it doesn't hurt to have an extra stud. The investment is rock-solid." His spiel ended on a crescendo of enthusiasm.

She didn't share his excitement. Hurt and anger swirled in her. "Why is the ranch suddenly so important to you, Tyler?'' she asked furiously. ''It wasn't so important when you took off nine years ago!''

''Landon left me half the ranch for a reason,'' he replied tightly.

''And you believe coming back and expanding the ranch's operations will make up for what happened in the past with Landon?''

Tyler looked away, not answering. He kicked at the dirt floor with the toe of his boot.

''Oh, Tyler,'' Brianne breathed, finally understanding what was driving him to succeed. She'd seen the pain in his eyes before he'd turned away. Stepping toward him, she placed a hand gently on his arm. The firm muscles beneath her palm bunched, and he turned his gaze on her.

''Nothing will change the past,'' she said softly, aching for him when she knew she shouldn't involve herself that way. ''And nothing will bring back Landon to give you a second chance. You need to find it in you to forgive yourself. Don't make the mistake of thinking a successful reining operating will make everything better.''

''It's not a mistake,'' he said evenly.

''Tyler, this is the only real home I've ever known and all me and my son have. I want to preserve as much of it as I can for him. I want Daniel to have everything I never had as a child. The security, hopes, dreams. A real place to call home. I won't risk losing it.''

Tyler heard the apprehension in her voice, saw the worry in her eyes. No matter what she'd done in the past, she honestly cared about the ranch. No greedy, selfish intentions for her; all she wanted was the promise of stability.

As he searched her warm eyes, the hard shell around his heart cracked. Maybe she'd had her own personal reasons for marrying Boyd that went beyond scheming, just as he'd had his own cause for leaving nine years ago. He put the interesting thought aside for the moment.

"I don't want to take the ranch away from you," he assured her. "I want the ranch to grow and prosper to its full potential." Without thinking, he reached up and touched his fingertips to her soft cheek, savoring the silken texture of her skin when she didn't pull away. "I know our past has been…uneasy at best, but we're partners. I wouldn't do anything to jeopardize the ranch."

The faintest glimmer of belief entered her gaze. Tyler realized he wanted her complete confidence. He *needed* her to believe in him because she'd been one of the people he'd disappointed in the past.

A new beginning, he thought.

His fingers feathered along her jaw, and she shivered. He cupped her face in his hands, forcing her to meet his gaze, desperate to persuade her. "Trust me, Brianne. Please."

Brianne knew Tyler wasn't going to give in on his decision. *He's a good man, missy. He's made a few mistakes in the past, but haven't we all?* Yes, she'd made her share of mistakes, and if she'd had the chance, she'd do plenty of things differently.

"Fine," she said, wishing Tyler would drop his hands from her face. "We'll purchase the stud."

He grinned broadly, and Brianne was mesmerized by how handsome Tyler looked when he was happy.

"Do you realize," he said in a low, playful growl, "that we've just made our first business decision together?"

More like he'd bulldozed her into agreeing. "Let's break out the champagne," she said in an attempt at humor while trying to ignore the heat in his eyes and the nearness of his body.

He winked at her. "We just might, honey."

Brianne's stomach tumbled at the silky endearment. The sweet feminine pull of awareness suddenly overwhelmed her. In the past three minutes something elemental had shifted between them. Something terrifying, exciting...and thrilling.

Transfixed by the desire in his gaze, Brianne couldn't obey the warning in her mind to step away. Even if she'd wanted to, she couldn't have moved. The hands on her face held her immobile. Tyler stared at her mouth, at the slow slide of his thumb skating across her bottom lip. Her lips parted and her breathing grew ragged. She longed for the forbidden.

Tyler knew what she wanted, and planned to give her just a taste of what her eyes begged for. Slowly, he lowered his head, brushing his mouth over hers in a gentle sigh of a kiss, teasing, but not quite applying enough pressure to make the kiss intimate.

Her hands landed on his chest, her fingers curling into him. A soft groan slipped past her lips. He smiled, but didn't take advantage of her offering, even as his hard body demanded he take action. No, it was enough that she wanted him.

Now he wanted her trust.

He pulled back, staring into her warm, limpid gaze. "Thank you, Bree. You won't regret the purchase, I promise."

It took all his willpower to step away when all he wanted was to haul her in his arms and kiss her senseless, and make them both forget about the mistakes and pain of the past. He knew how good it could be between them, how sweet and drugging and wild she could be when he touched her a certain way.

One day at a time, he recited silently, and hoped his patience held out.

He smiled at her. "I'll call Armon tomorrow. With

any luck we can cut a deal and pick up Roman Warrior this weekend.''

Tyler walked into the kitchen Friday evening and found Brianne standing at the counter making a green salad for dinner and Daniel setting the table. He removed his hat, dropped it on the hatrack in the corner, and shoved his fingers through his hair.

"Roman Warrior's ours," he said triumphantly, having just sealed the deal with Armon after a day of negotiating.

He waited for Brianne to acknowledge him, or the announcement, but she seemed intent on shredding a head of lettuce to tiny, minuscule pieces. Her lack of enthusiasm didn't surprise him, considering how opposed she'd been to the whole idea of acquiring a champion reining horse. He reminded himself to be patient, and give her time to get used to the concept.

"Who's Roman Warrior?" Daniel asked curiously.

"He's a champion reining horse, and your mother and I bought him."

"Cool," Daniel said, smiling.

"It's *totally* cool," he agreed, grinning back at the boy. Moving to the spot next to Brianne, he settled his hip against the counter and openly watched her.

She'd changed out of the work clothes she'd worn that afternoon to help clean out the paddocks. A little over an hour ago she'd been head-to-toe dusty and sweaty. Now her skin looked freshly scrubbed, and she smelled powdery and feminine. A pink, sleeveless summer dress accentuated the indentation of her waist and the flare of her hips. Her legs were bare, as were her feet. She'd unbraided her hair, securing the wavy blond strands at her nape with a gold hairclip, not the silver one he'd given her.

She looked young, fresh, sexy as hell, and all he could think about was slowly slipping open the imitation pearl buttons marching so primly down the front of her dress and revealing more smooth skin.

Banishing the arousing images before his body responded, he grabbed a radish and crunched into it. "So, what do you think, Bree?"

The knife in her hands sliced quickly through the radishes, coming dangerously close to her fingers. "Armon actually agreed to thirty thousand?"

A wry smile canted his mouth. "Don't sound so disappointed."

"I'm just surprised," she said, her light tone covering up the lie. She dumped the radish slices into the bowl of lettuce and started whittling away at the mushrooms. "You've been haggling with him all day. I was beginning to think he wasn't going to bend."

She'd been *hoping*, Tyler knew, and understood her apprehension. "Armon likes to haggle. He'll grumble and complain that we're robbin' him blind, but he's really a pushover. One of the nicest guys you'll ever meet."

"When is Roman Warrior coming?" Daniel asked, excitement gathering in his voice.

"We can pick him up this weekend," he told Daniel, then transferred his gaze back to Brianne, who was slicing a mushroom with all the concentration of a neurosurgeon. She tossed the remains into the lettuce, then rinsed her hands. "Whadaya say, Bree?"

She flitted away from him, her expression noncommittal. Thrusting her hand into a quilted mitt, she pulled a steaming pan of meat loaf from the oven. Delicious smells wafted in the air. "I'll have a private paddock waiting for him when he gets here."

"You're coming with me to pick up Roman Warrior,

Brianne," Tyler told her. Picking up the bowl of salad, he carried it to the table.

She placed the platter of meatloaf next to the salad. "No, I'm not," she said emphatically.

He met her gaze, undaunted by the fire sparking in the golden depths. "Yes, you are," he opposed just as firmly.

Her lips pursed in annoyance. "Tyler, I can't just take off for Oregon. I have a business to run—"

"Jasper can handle things for two days," he argued. "It's only an eight-hour drive. We'll leave tomorrow morning and be home by Sunday evening."

Her eyes widened, her mind registering the implications of being alone with him for two days. "I can't leave Daniel—"

"Jasper said Betty wouldn't mind coming over and watching him," he replied, squashing her argument.

"You asked?"

"I didn't *ask.* Jasper offered, I considered, and Betty agreed without much prompting."

Her chin lifted. "Seems like you've thought of everything."

Everything but what to do about the burning desire she inflamed in him. On impulse, he touched her, gently curling his fingers around her upper arms. Unidentifiable emotions smoldered in her eyes. She attempted to step away, but he wouldn't allow her to escape. At least not yet. He caught Daniel frowning at him, but his only thought was to calm Brianne, soothe her worries and try to convince her he wasn't the threat she believed him to be.

"Look, I know how nervous you are about purchasing Roman Warrior," he began, infusing his voice with sincerity. "I want you to come with me, meet Armon Eckerly, and see what kind of quality horses he breeds."

"I trust your judgment," she said tightly.

She didn't. Not really. Obstinate woman, he thought, torn between shaking some sense into her, and kissing her mindless. "I want you to see Roman Warrior first-hand, before we hand over any cash. If you aren't thoroughly impressed, we'll reconsider."

Her gaze narrowed, a direct contradiction to the tension ebbing from her body. "You would do that?"

He put on his best poker face, confident once she saw how magnificent Roman Warrior was, she'd be just as excited as he was. "Absolutely."

She stared at him for a long moment, wariness deepening the shade of her eyes. "Can I talk to you for a moment?"

His mouth quirked. "I thought that's what we were doing."

"Alone," she said purposefully. "In the other room."

Away from prying eyes and ears, he realized. Apparently, the storm hadn't finished its tempest. He nodded, and after Brianne instructed Daniel to finish setting the table, he followed her into the living room.

She snapped on the lamp next to the couch, illuminating the room, then put the physical barrier of the coffee table between them. Halting by the recliner, she turned and faced him, her eyes hazed with confusion.

"Why are you doing this?" she asked, folding her arms across her chest and absently rubbing the spot on her arms where his hands had caressed minutes before.

He grappled for the patience he seemed to be needing as much as oxygen these days. "Why am I doing what, Bree? Being so nice?"

A flood of scarlet poured across her cheeks. "Well, yes."

"You accused me of the same thing the day after I arrived." He gave her a lopsided smile designed to put her at ease. "You make *nice* seem like a plague. I'm not the miscreant you think I am."

Something in her eyes softened, but her stance remained unyielding. "I don't think you're a miscreant, but after our original discussion about Roman Warrior, and your insistence to buy him, you're being awfully accommodating."

"We're partners, a team," he said, leisurely moving around the coffee table toward her.

She watched him with all the trepidation of a trapped mouse keeping an eye on a hungry cat. "I was under the impression that didn't make any difference to your 'plans.'"

"It does make a difference, Brianne. I need your cooperation in order for this venture to be successful. For both of us. I don't want to be the enemy, so quit making me one."

Her shoulders slumped. "I never meant to imply you were the enemy."

Yes, she had, because in her mind he *was* the rival. Their conversation the other day had brought that fact into light. She believed he would seize the security she'd created for her and Daniel. He wasn't that heartless, despite past hurt and anger. He only wanted the inheritance that belonged to him.

He rubbed a hand over the tight muscles along his shoulder and neck. "The past is the past, Brianne," he said quietly. "I've wasted enough years with regrets. I'm determined to make the reining operation work, and I want your opinion and involvement in the process."

Brianne stared at the earnest expression on Tyler's face, the solemnity in his eyes, and wanted so badly to believe his words, trust him even. Old habits and heartbreak died hard, though, and she couldn't bring herself to give him that much of the independent person she'd become over the years. Not when she had so much at stake.

Tyler slung an arm over her shoulder and gave her a light squeeze, more affectionate than sexual. "C'mon, Bree, say you'll go with me to Oregon. From what Jasper tells me, you haven't had a vacation in three years."

Longer than that, she thought, unable to recall any kind of real vacation in her lifetime. She slanted him a stern look, her stomach tumbling when she realized the close proximity of his face to hers. Two inches forward and his lips would graze hers. The arm around her gave her a sense of comfort she hadn't experienced in what seemed like an eternity. All an illusion, she knew, knowing she'd be foolish to depend on Tyler for even something as simple as comfort.

"I don't need a vacation," she told him, ducking from under his arm. "I can't *afford* a vacation, not if we're going to buy Roman Warrior."

He rolled his eyes dramatically. "God, Brianne, don't you ever let down that guard of yours?"

Not often, and not around you, she thought desperately.

"Can't you just do something for yourself? For the good of the ranch, even?" He didn't give her a chance to answer before he plowed on. "It'll be strictly business. And you have to admit it would be nice to get away for a couple of days."

She hesitated. "I don't know—"

"You're coming with me, even if I have to bind and gag you," he insisted. "Your opinion and approval *does* matter. I don't want this to be a constant source of contention between us."

His debate chipped away at her resolve, made her want to do something as carefree and spontaneous as take off for Oregon for the weekend. She chewed on her thumbnail, contemplating the pros and cons of accompanying him on the trip. She'd never left Daniel before, and just the thought of being alone with Tyler was enough to make her pulse race.

She didn't want to support a deal so certain to shake up the stability and security of the ranch, yet this purchase was so important to Tyler. He looked so expectant and hopeful she knew she'd crush him if she refused. She shouldn't care, but she did. She always would.

She damned her treacherous heart.

"Say you'll go, Bree," Tyler coaxed softly.

"Go ahead and go, Mom." Daniel's voice sounded from the far end of the room. "I'll be fine."

Brianne spun around, surprised to see Daniel standing in the doorway leading from the kitchen, and more shocked by his soft-spoken announcement. She wondered how long he'd been standing there, and how much of her argument with Tyler he'd witnessed.

Daniel moved into the room, his expression reserved as he glanced from Tyler to Brianne.

The past week, and Tyler's attention, had wrought a dramatic transformation over her son. Daniel was slowly coming to accept Tyler, his real father, in his life. The notion frightened Brianne when it should have pleased her. Just because Tyler insisted the ranch was what he wanted, there were no guarantees he'd be around in the months to come. Accepting Tyler as a partner was beyond her control. Her son's fate was not, and she'd do whatever necessary to shield him from further pain. Even withhold the truth of his parentage, no matter how much the guilt ate at her.

Daniel shifted on his feet, clearly uneasy under his mother's scrutiny. "Really, Mom, it's okay if you go."

"You're sure?" she asked, carefully gauging his expression.

He glanced at Tyler as if sizing him up, then back at Brianne. The faintest hint of trust shimmered in Daniel's dark blue eyes, and Brianne's heart lurched in her chest.

"Yeah, I'm sure." His voice rang with a confidence Brianne hadn't heard in a long time. "I'm not a baby, Mom. Besides, how can you buy a horse you've never seen before?"

Tyler chuckled and clasped his hand on Daniel's shoulder in an open display of affection. "That's exactly what I've been trying to tell her, sport."

"You're sure it's not an inconvenience for Betty to stay here?" she asked.

"Jasper said she'd love to stay with Daniel," Tyler confirmed once again.

Brianne pulled in a deep breath, feeling like she was taking a dive off a steep cliff, with nothing to break her fall. "I guess I'm outnumbered two to one."

Victory gleamed in Tyler's eyes. "I like a woman who knows when to surrender."

She lifted her chin primly. "I'm only agreeing to accompany you because it'll be in the best interest of the ranch."

A maddeningly wicked smile spread across Tyler's handsome face. "Of course."

CHAPTER EIGHT

"WHY did you marry him?"

Tyler's question penetrated the silence enveloping the cab of his truck as they headed toward Oregon to pick up Roman Warrior. Brianne didn't have to ask who or what he was talking about, but formulating a plausible answer was a bit more difficult.

The most obvious reasons for her spontaneous marriage to Boyd swamped Brianne. She'd been young, pregnant and frightened, and when Tyler didn't return to marry her as he'd promised, she did the only thing a despairing eighteen-year-old girl could to offer her baby, *his* baby, a better way of life than what she could have provided for it.

"Brianne?"

Knowing there was no way to avoid the inevitable discussion, not when she was trapped in a vehicle with him for hours, she rolled her head against the back of her seat, away from the passing scenery, and met his gaze. The look in his blue eyes struggled to understand her motives for what she'd done.

She drew a deep breath, mentally editing the truth for Tyler. "I was so scared after you left," she said. "You never called or wrote to tell me where you were. I didn't think you were coming back. Boyd told me you *weren't* coming back, and I was naive enough to believe him.

"My father..." She swallowed the bitter words, *My father didn't want to have anything to do with me or your baby,* and continued. "He wanted to move on to North Dakota, and I didn't want to go with him. We were never close, and there was nothing in North Dakota for me. But I didn't have anything of my own, either. No job. No money, and I did the only thing I could think of at the time.

"When Boyd offered to marry me, I accepted, hoping for a better way of life." It was all truth, minus a pregnancy that Boyd resented from the very first. And as the years passed and she was unable to conceive *Boyd's* child, a legitimate child that would inherit Whitmore Acres over Tyler's son, his bitterness and hatred had compounded. And Daniel had ultimately paid the price.

She shivered, recalling how much Boyd resented Daniel being Tyler's son, and how he'd scorned the young, hopeful boy who'd wanted so badly to please the man he believed was his "dad." Her heart twisted painfully at the memory of Daniel's crestfallen hopes, and the eventual lack of self-confidence instilled by Boyd's neglect.

"Where is your father now?" Tyler asked, bringing her back to the present.

"I don't know. He moved after I married Boyd. He always did hold a grudge against the Whitmores after your father fired him for his drinking problem. I haven't heard from him since the day he left."

Tyler's sapphire gaze bore into hers, searching deep. His fingers tightened on the steering wheel. "Did you love him?"

"My father?" She lifted a brow in surprise to his question. "Of course I did—"

"No, Boyd." His tone was impatient, his body suddenly radiating a palpable tension.

"No, Tyler." Her answer was honest and straight from the heart. "And he didn't love me, either. He only wanted me because I belonged to you. He knew if you ever came back and found me married to him it would hurt you. And it worked.''

A muscle in Tyler's jaw clenched. "Yes, it did.''

Tyler fixed his gaze on the stretch of road in front of them, battling with the tumult of emotions clamoring inside him. Anger steamed in him for falling victim to his half-brother's cunning, instead of fighting for what was his. The reining operation. And Brianne.

Would the regret and guilt ever stop eating at him? *Only when you put the past to rest,* whispered his conscience. But how, he wondered.

"It wasn't a happy marriage," she said, snagging his attention once again with her softly spoken statement. "Far from it.''

"Did he…'' He swallowed hard, the unpleasant thoughts he wanted to express choking him. "Did he abuse you?''

"Not physically, though as you know he had a violent temper, and sometimes his words cut deeper than a knife.'' Her mouth curled into a caustic smile. "When he was in one of his moods, or drunk, I'd try to avoid him and keep Daniel out of his way.''

Tyler suddenly understood how Boyd's manipulation had shaped her into the strong, self-sufficient woman she was today. Understanding, too, Daniel's initial hostile reaction to him when he'd learned he was Boyd's brother. Both mother and son hadn't had much reason to trust in their lifetime.

It seemed she'd paid an astronomical price for what she'd acquired.

"Boyd was so bitter and spiteful," Brianne continued. Now that they were talking about the past, and doing so civilly, she wanted to purge all the ugliness she'd kept buried for so long. "He found fault in everything, and nothing made him happy. He spent most of his time at the bar drinking instead of facing the problems at home." And spent a lot of nights away from home. But his absence had been a salvation for her. "One night he came home drunk and belligerent, ranting about you, Landon, and the will he'd left behind, and how *everything* should have been his." The tirade was nothing new. She'd grown used to Boyd's nasty accusations and insults, and the hateful allegation that Daniel was nothing more than the bastard his *real* father was. "The intensity of his hatred was frightening," she whispered.

"What happened, Brianne?" Tyler asked, as if sensing there was more.

She rubbed her arms to ward off a sudden chill in the cab. "He left the house in a rage. That was the night he died."

"Jesus, Brianne," he breathed, his expression grim. "I didn't realize it had been so bad."

How could he have possibly known the extent of her suffering when he'd never come back for her as she'd hoped and prayed he would, forcing her to make choices that had altered her entire life. "There's a price to pay for everything, isn't there, Tyler?"

Her soft-spoken question startled Tyler. He kneaded the taut muscles at the nape of his neck, reflecting on the huge price his own isolation had cost him over the years. The loss of Landon's respect. A life without Brianne. "I guess we've both paid some hefty fines, haven't we?"

A ghost of a smile touched her lips. "Yes, we have."

He reached out and touched her cheek, her skin soft and warm and vibrant beneath his fingertips. "I'm sorry," he said gruffly. *For so many things.*

"So am I, Tyler," she whispered, a sad, emotion-filled sigh escaping her. "So am I."

"He's magnificent, isn't he?"

Brianne smiled at the pride in Armon Eckerly's voice as she watched Tyler ride Roman Warrior in one of the corrals. Armon's comment could have applied to the man astride the horse, or the horse itself. Both were superb specimens of their breed. Lean, powerful, and breathtakingly magnificent. Horse and rider flowed together despite the difficult exercises Tyler executed, as if they'd been custom made for each other.

Leaning her forearms on the wood fence, she glanced at the older man. Armon Eckerly's short, round frame was stuffed into a Western shirt, Wrangler jeans and cowboy boots too gleaming to have seen a hard day's work. Sprigs of gray could be detected beneath his immaculate beige Stetson, and his light blue eyes winked with country hospitality. Brianne had instantly liked the older man. It was obvious by the boisterous reception and hearty handshake Armon had welcomed Tyler with, he held Tyler in high regard.

"I don't know much about reining," she admitted, watching as Tyler maneuvered Roman Warrior in a series of demanding patterns. He brought Roman to a sliding stop, then whirled him around smoothly, efficiently, without breaking their rhythm or faltering on form. "But I do know quarter horses. Roman Warrior has a strong conformation."

"That he does," Armon said on a hearty laugh. "Those powerful hindquarters of his are his trademark. Tyler's had his eye on Roman since the day he came to work for me. Fact is, I'm glad Tyler's purchasing him. That horse responds to him like no other trainer I've employed. You're lucky to have a man of Tyler's skill and patience to work your horses. I don't doubt he'll have a nice reining operation going before long."

Brianne didn't doubt it, either, since Tyler was so

driven to enforce the program. Before she could comment on Armon's appreciation of Tyler, the object of their discussion brought Roman Warrior to an abrupt halt mere feet from them. A huge swirl of dust accompanied the stop. Roman snorted and shook his big head.

Roman Warrior was, indeed, a glorious animal.

Tyler dismounted fluidly and handed the reins to a nearby ranch hand. A huge grin split his handsome features as he sauntered out the corral gate and toward her, his stride lazy.

Stopping in front of her, he pushed back his hat, revealing eyes full of excitement...and reserved anticipation. "What do you think?" he asked.

Brianne was impressed and convinced. From a business perspective, she'd decided a horse of Roman Warrior's quality might be a good thing after all, and something she could handle on her own, if necessary. If anything, Roman Warrior would be a profitable stud.

Now, Tyler wanted her approval. The hope in his voice asked for it. The expectation in the taut line of his body told her how vital her positive response was to him. She couldn't disappoint him.

"I think," she said on a dramatic sigh that drew out the moment, "we just bought ourselves a reining champion."

Tyler's smile widened into a dazzling grin. His arms suddenly went around her, gathering her close and lifting her off the ground. He made a wild cowboy hoot of triumph and spun her around.

She laughed, enjoying herself and Tyler way too much. She became light-headed, from the spin and the man who crushed her to his lean, muscular body.

He stopped and slid her slowly down the length of him, until her boots touched the ground again. The friction of hard male planes against soft feminine contours started flashfires streaking up her thighs, across her belly and over the sensitive tips of her breasts. She was breathless and slightly aroused by the time he released her.

"Thank you, Brianne," he said, his voice low and husky. "You won't regret this."

"How about you two stay for dinner?" Armon suggested jovially. "I can have Fran put two extra plates on the table."

Tyler's gaze never left Brianne's. "I think we're going to go out and celebrate." His words were innocent, but the heat in his eyes was not.

"Good idea," Armon said, not at all offended by Tyler's refusal. "You two have a lot to celebrate."

"That we do," Tyler murmured.

An hour later, after signing the papers that made them legal owners of Roman Warrior, Armon walked with them back to Tyler's truck.

"We'll leave the trailer here and pick up Roman Warrior early tomorrow morning," Tyler told Armon.

"He'll be ready," Armon promised, pumping Tyler's hand in a congratulatory shake. "And if you ever need a job, you know you've always got one with me."

"Thanks for the offer," Tyler said, withdrawing the truck keys from his jean pocket and sliding his gaze to Brianne. "But I don't plan on going anywhere anytime soon."

Tyler paced the confines of his motel room, the exhilaration over the day's events keeping him on a natural high.

Strolling to the window overlooking the parking lot, he braced a forearm on the cool surface and stared at nothing in particular, his thoughts lost on the woman occupying the room next to his. He'd told her he'd pick her up at seven to give her time to rest, shower and change. He'd already taken his own shower and still had another hour left to kill. Restless energy buzzed through his body, making a brief nap impossible.

After so many years of bitter emotions, he'd never expected Brianne's approval of Roman Warrior to mean so much to him, but it had. When he first returned to Whitmore Acres his sole purpose was to achieve his own personal goals, regardless of Brianne's thoughts or feelings on the matter.

Somewhere along the way that had changed. Somewhere along the way he began to care again and see her in a different light than what he'd believed for nine years. This morning's discussion about Boyd, and her reasons for marrying him, had softened a part of him that had been hardened to any feelings for her.

Absently rubbing his thumb along the faint stubble lining his jaw, he reflected on his stormy relationship with Brianne. Idly, he wondered if there was anything left between them worth salvaging. They'd both endured so much pain and heartache. Was there even a scrap of hope or trust they could build into something more promising?

Grabbing the remote on his way to the queen-size bed dominating the small room, he propped himself against the headboard and flipped on the TV. A weatherman on a local station forecasted sunny skies for the following day, but Tyler only listened with half an ear.

He'd thought a lot about the discussion he'd had with Brianne about Landon. The words she'd spoken, *No matter what you believe, he loved you like you were his own son. That's as close to being a father as it gets,* had haunted him during the day. And in the quiet of the night, he'd tossed those words around in his mind, analyzing them and eventually believing them. Brianne had been right. It didn't matter that his blood wasn't pure

Whitmore. In his heart, he was a Whitmore from the moment Landon had accepted him as one.

He switched off the TV and sat in the dark room, wondering if he could make things up to someone who was dead and gone. Were all his efforts to utilize his inheritance and run a successful reining operation a waste?

You need to find it in you to forgive yourself. Brianne's words echoed through him, weaving around a soul battered and bruised from years of self-recriminations. He needed to make peace with Landon, and himself. Yet the only way he'd find peace was with the ranch, working to compensate for all the lost, lonely years he'd accumulated.

Shaking off the troubling thoughts, he stood, determined to move forward and finally unchain the demons he'd dragged around for nine endless years. He concentrated on all the good things that had happened since he'd come home. There were plenty of things to celebrate, most recently the purchase of Roman Warrior.

With that last thought nudging his mind, he picked up his truck keys from the dresser and headed out the door with a smile and a plan to tackle Brianne's resistance.

A winning smile and a convincing story of how he'd locked his key in his hotel room produced Tyler a key to Brianne's room. Lucky for him, he'd registered both rooms under his name, and the young, pretty clerk had been more than eager to accommodate him.

Tucking the key into his pocket, he quietly closed Brianne's door, shrouding him in the dark shadows of nightfall. His luck held out. Beyond the bathroom door the shower ran, affording him the few minutes he needed to set up their "celebration."

Ten minutes later, settled at the head of Brianne's bed

with a bottle of convenience store champagne nestled in a cheap plastic ice bucket on the nightstand, Tyler waited for Brianne. She finally emerged from the bathroom, skin flushed from her shower, a billow of steam trailing her. She wore a pair of tight-fitting jeans and a white camisole that clung to her damp skin, hinting at the generous curves of her breasts.

Except for the slice of light coming from the bathroom, the room was dim and she didn't notice him. He didn't mind. It gave him a handful of seconds to look his fill before she discovered him.

Walking to the dresser, she peered into the attached mirror, unable to see him in the reflection. She fussed with her make-up, sweeping a stroke of blush over her cheeks and adding a sheen of gloss to her lips. Lifting her arms, she unpinned the hair piled on her head. Unrestrained breasts swayed with the movement, the pebbled tips straining against the thin cotton. She shook her head, tumbling the damp strands down her back before she began pulling a brush through the thick mass.

Tyler dragged in a deep breath, his body and mind seduced by the uninhibited sensuality of her movements. There was none of the reserve she tried so hard to maintain around him. Just a natural femininity that he responded to on a basic level. This is how he wanted her, soft and willing, with all barriers swept away.

Humming a light tune, she gathered her hair into a fist and grabbed the silver and turquoise clip he'd given her.

"Leave it down," Tyler said on impulse, his voice husky and rough.

She spun around on a gasp. The clip slipped from her fingers and fell to the carpeting. Eyes wide, she pressed a hand to her heart, her gaze searching the dim room.

Finding him, her lips pursed into a thin line, barely suppressing the outrage simmering in her eyes.

"Dammit, Tyler, you scared the life out of me!" Snatching the clip from the floor, she defiantly secured her hair back before giving him the full force of her irritation. "What are you doing in *my* room?"

"I bought some champagne." Swinging his legs over the side of the bed, he lifted the bottle from the ice and started twisting off the wire casing. "Nothing fancy. I just wanted to propose a toast to our new investment."

She snapped on the nearest lamp, flooding the room in a bright glow and dispelling the cloak of shadowed intimacy. "We could have ordered a bottle of champagne at the restaurant," she said, some of the heat leaving her voice.

This was a personal, private celebration. "We can do that, too." The plastic cork popped with his prodding, skyrocketing toward the ceiling. He chuckled when she ducked at the explosion.

She glared back, the scowl lacking any real intensity. "How did you get in here?"

He poured the bubbly liquid into two plastic cups, then glanced at her, a smile tipping his mouth. "A man has his ways."

"I'll just bet," Brianne murmured derisively. That smile alone would gain him access to her room key, and anything else he might request.

Standing, he held out a glass of champagne, silently daring her to come closer. "Here you go."

His voice was low and intimate, doing dangerous, melting things to her insides. Grabbing her blouse off the end of the mattress, she thrust her arms through the short sleeves in an attempt to protect herself from such responses. Cautiously, she ventured to his side of the bed.

"One drink," she said sternly. She didn't want to spoil his good mood, but being alone with him, with a swirling awareness charging the air between them and a huge, empty bed waiting to be rumpled by lovers wasn't a smart idea. The sooner they left for dinner, the better.

"One drink," he agreed, his fingers brushing hers as he pushed the cup into her hand. "To a fresh start," he toasted, tapping his champagne to hers. "A new beginning."

His all-consuming expression told her he meant the vow. She shivered, knowing the secret standing between them made any hope for a future impossible. There were so many emotional obstacles blocking their way to true happiness, she wasn't even certain he'd stick around long enough to work at a new beginning.

"To Roman Warrior," she rebutted, taking a swallow of champagne.

"To *us*," he said, his tone fiercely possessive.

"Don't," she managed, struggling against the softening emotions threatening her. "It won't work between us." *I can't allow you to get that close!*

Tyler's fingers tightened around his cup until the plastic cracked. She was giving up, walking away without trying to bridge the chasm of old hurt keeping them separated. Determination rippled through him. He was going to make the first attempt at healing old pains, starting with putting the past to rest.

With that decision, he placed his champagne on the nightstand, ignoring the wariness creasing her brow. "I don't want Boyd between us anymore."

Surprise lit her eyes for a brief second before regret clouded the brilliance. She set her cup next to his and skirted away from him. "He'll always be between us, and you'll always resent me for marrying him."

He shook his head, searching for a way to breach the

walls she shoved up quicker than he could tear them down. Trust. He needed to gain her trust. But dammit, how did he accomplish his goal when she bolted like a frightened deer whenever he broached issues that needed to be discussed in order for them to go forward?

"I understand *why* you married Boyd," he countered, allowing none of his frustration to edge into his tone.

Brianne closed her eyes, wishing he *did* know the true reason she'd given in to such desperation as to marry someone she didn't love. Her teeth sank into her bottom lip, biting back the truth rising swiftly to the surface.

His warm fingers slid along her jaw, and she blinked her eyes open, staring into the midnight depths of his gaze. A fierce glow kindled there, a mixture of staunch perseverance, desire and a need that rushed through her own blood.

"I won't deny I always believed you married Boyd to gain Whitmore Acres," he began, his thumbs caressing her cheeks, his eyes never leaving hers. "I couldn't think of any other reason why you'd sacrifice yourself to him. But I'm half to blame for you marrying him."

"Tyler—"

He pressed his fingers to her lips. "Let me finish. Please. I didn't stop to think about you being all alone with your father, and not knowing where I'd gone or if I was ever coming back. I didn't think about anyone, or anything, but myself. Can you forgive me for leaving you the way I did?"

"Forgive you?" she choked. "Oh, Tyler. I was hurt and angry, but I never condemned you for what you did."

But he'd hurt her, Tyler thought. Badly. The chain of events resulting from him leaving had ruined so many lives, and affected both of them still. "Then maybe, somehow, we can try and repair the damage of the past. Build a future..."

She manacled his wrists, intending to pull his hands away from her face, but he held tight. Didn't he understand that they had no future, just a tangled past that would forever be a wedge between them? "It's too late to start over, and involvement would only complicate our business relationship."

Tyler didn't think so. It could only enhance what they shared. Except she was too damned stubborn to see that. Too damned frightened to trust him.

"We're already involved, Bree," he said, moving closer, bridging the physical distance between them until their thighs skimmed. Her breath caught in her throat and she jerked back, but the hands spanning her jaw kept her right where he wanted her.

"Things are changing between us," he murmured. "I know it, you know it. The only question left is, what are *we* going to do about it?"

"Absolutely nothing," Brianne whispered despairingly, aching for what could never be. They could never recapture the innocent, youthful love they'd shared, the hopes and dreams that had been crushed by the cruelty of one man.

"Wrong answer," he said softly, drawing her face closer with the pressure of his palms on her jaw. His heavy-lidded gaze glittered with masculine purpose. "This is what I think we should do about it," he muttered, seconds before dropping his mouth over hers.

Tyler's kiss was bold and greedy, robbing Brianne of sanity or will. A heaviness settled in her breasts, and the tips tightened into hard beads that ached for his touch.

Shocked by her response, her hands landed on his chest to push him away, to escape the sweet, drugging awareness and need. But her heart had a mind of its own, and it slowly opened to receive the tenderness Tyler had to offer.

"Tyler," she groaned uncertainly. Lord help her, she couldn't resist him. Sensations bloomed inside her, awakening desires that had lain dormant for an eternity. Despite everything between them, he was the only man she craved, the only man who made her feel alive and desirable.

"Shh," Tyler hushed against her parted lips as his fingers fumbled with the buttons on her shirt. Once open, he shoved the garment down her arms, leaving her clad in her thin camisole. Then he was kissing her again, lips and tongue teasing her deliciously. His hands roamed down her spine and over her bottom. Pulling her hips to his, he moved them in a slow, intimate rhythm.

Her breath caught in her throat and her head spun. He kissed her until she trembled, until a rising hunger and need overwhelmed her and she clung to him. Her body rubbed against his, seeking his warmth and strength and touch. He gave her all three.

He slowly guided her backward, toward the bed, his mouth playing seductively over hers. The backs of her knees collided with the edge, and she clutched her hands around his neck to keep from tumbling back.

She fell anyway, sinking into the mattress with his hard body blanketing her. Her thighs parted, welcoming him, and he automatically settled his hips in that natural harbor.

He yanked his shirt over his head and tossed it aside. She touched him, sliding her hands over warm, honed flesh. His eyes blazed with desire and a powerful, unbridled need that echoed in her heart. He unclipped her hair, tossed the barrette aside, and spread the shimmering strands around her head.

"I want you, Bree," he said huskily, threading his

callused fingers through the mass of silk. "Do you want me?"

She ran her tongue over her bottom lip, incapable of lying when her body trembled for him. "Yes." Oh, God, she'd *never* stopped wanting him.

Tyler pulled in a deep breath to steady the sudden pounding of his heart. The honesty in that one word, the trust, was his undoing. He hesitated, his heart suddenly swelling with emotions too intense to analyze at a time like this. Brushing strands of hair from her flushed face, he saw a woman who made him whole and complete. A woman who'd haunted him for the past nine years. The only woman he'd ever wanted.

"Then kiss me like you mean it," he said softly.

To Tyler's surprise, and satisfaction, she accepted the sexy challenge. Sliding her fingers into his hair, she pulled his mouth to hers. This was no tentative meeting of lips. She delivered a hot, openmouthed kiss, like a woman starved for the taste of her man. He savored the faint taste of champagne, and a wild desperation. Responding on a primitive level, he deepened the kiss even more, giving as good as she gave. His hand covered her breast, squeezing the mound through the annoying obstruction of her camisole. She arched into his palm, a moan of frustration vibrating in her throat.

"It's okay, baby," he murmured against her lips. Pulling the hem of her top from her jeans, he drew the garment over her head, trapping her hands above her for a moment in the tangle of material so he could admire the full swells of her breasts.

Her luminous gaze widened, and a flush stole over her face. Dipping his head, he stroked his tongue over a nipple, then blew a hot stream of breath over the hardened tip. He released her hands and met her bright gaze, shimmering with desire and need. Silently, he dared her to be as bold as he. No restraint, no withholding anything.

She whispered his name, the sweetest sound he'd ever heard, and slowly, shamelessly pulled his head down to the tight crests begging for his attention. His mouth closed over a nipple, his tongue flicking over the beaded tip before he suckled her deep into his mouth. With a low moan, she held him to her breast.

"Brianne." Her name was a groan on his lips. His mouth lifted from her breasts and skimmed upward. A soft, arousing sound escaped her, and she arched her neck, giving his damp, marauding mouth better access to her throat. His lips slid along her jaw, then crushed against her mouth in a hungry assault, his tongue delving and tangling with hers. His body rocked against hers, slow and easy, until natural instinct took over and his thrusts became more urgent, more demanding.

Impatient for her, and hating the denim separating them, he skimmed his fingers over the waistband of her jeans, finding and unsnapping the front closure.

The touch of Tyler's palm smoothing over her belly, pushing aside her jeans, brought Brianne out of the sensual haze fogging her mind and clouding her judgment. She caught his wrist just as his hand skimmed the lace band of her panties. He immediately stopped his quest and met her gaze.

Brianne stared into Tyler's dark eyes, blazing with a need as fierce as the one pulsing through her body. And in that moment she knew if they made love, she'd not only give him her body, but her heart and soul, too.

It couldn't happen. Passion and desire had a tendency to soften anger and resentments, but how long would it be before Tyler remembered the ugly past dividing them?

"Brianne?" Tyler's voice was strung as taut as his body.

A painful rush of breath escaped her. "Tyler, we can't—"

"Oh, yes, we can," he murmured silkily, dipping his head to drop soft, teasing kisses on the corner of her mouth. Freeing his hand from hers, he palmed the heavy weight of her breast, his thumb flicking over the tight center. He smiled against her lips when she issued a moan.

"Tyler." Her voice was breathy, and she tried to clear the desire and longing from her throat as her hands pushed against his shoulders. "Don't make this any harder than it already is."

He lifted his head, a wicked smile curving his lips. "Harder wouldn't be such a bad thing, darlin'."

She groaned at his pun, and shored up every last reserve of determination to fight him off. "Tyler, no!" she said through gritted teeth.

That got his attention, and he suddenly frowned at her. "No?"

He seemed so surprised, and confused, she nearly laughed. "No. We can't do this. We can't...have sex."

"Sex," he repeatedly flatly, disgust in his tone. He moved off her, but his irritated gaze kept her nailed to the spot. "Is that what you think this was all about? Gratuitous sex? A wham-bam-thank-you-ma'am kind of romp?"

She scrambled off the bed and quickly zipped her jeans and donned her camisole. "I call it a mistake." A lie, but a necessary one to keep the needed distance between them.

"Like hell it was," he growled, his expression darkening with anger. "I don't recall forcing you to kiss me.

In fact, I distinctly remember you pulling my mouth to your brea—''

"Stop," she choked, mortified that his mere words had the ability to make her breasts swell and tingle against her camisole.

Tyler sat up at the side of the bed, swearing bluntly as he dragged his hands through his hair. He'd pushed her too far too fast, but damn, she'd been warm and willing...then ice cold. He didn't understand what had gone wrong.

Just moments ago he'd felt something with Brianne. Not just physical desire, but a ray of tender emotions still simmering between them. Buried beneath the old bitterness and hurt, he'd glimpsed fragments of the love and gentleness that had brought them together in their youth.

"Tyler," she began, her voice imploring him to understand. "Everything is happening too fast. I'm not ready for this. For us. Can't we just be friends?"

"Friends?" He barked an incredulous laugh. Unable to help himself, he raked the length of her with a searing look. "Lady, 'friends' don't do the things we just did."

Face flushing, she averted her gaze and began putting the cosmetics scattered on the dresser into a makeup bag. "Tyler, don't make this so difficult, please."

"*I'm* making this difficult?" He stood and approached her, shaking his head, wishing he could shake the irritation weaving through him just as easily. "You're the one who wants to be friends after what just happened on that bed."

Her spine stiffened, her gaze meeting his in the mirror's reflection. "What's so bad about being friends?"

He jammed his hands on his hips, piercing her with his gaze. "*Friends* don't kiss like they can't get enough of each other. A *friend* wouldn't want to strip you naked, push you back on that mattress and *make love* to you until we were both so crazed with pleasure you'd forget the meaning of 'friends.'" Her eyes widened at his blunt monologue, but he didn't care because the words painted a vivid picture that made her realize exactly how far they'd nearly gone. "I think somewhere along the way we bypassed friendship."

"Then maybe that's where we ought to start," she said quietly, turning to face him, her chin tilted at a defiant angle. "Business partners should be friends."

Despite her stubborn stance, he saw the vulnerability shining in her eyes and that damnable fear he'd yet to unearth. A defeated sigh unraveled from his lungs.

He needed her trust. Without it they had no hope for a future. And if trust started with her platonic version of friendship, he'd forsake physical intimacy with her to gain the emotional closeness that would give him insight to her fears.

He dragged a hand over his jaw, feeling ragged from the inside out. "All right, we'll do it your way."

CHAPTER NINE

BRIANNE was back to baking. With a vengeance.

Today marked a week since the incident in the motel room. Seven days since Tyler had branded her his. One hundred and sixty-eight hours since he'd last touched her, kissed her, caressed her.

Her body still burned from the heat of his touch.

Retrieving a pan of cinnamon sugar cookies from the oven and placing it on the stove top, she removed her mitt and tossed it on the counter. She pulled in a deep breath, but it did nothing to ease the tightness in the vicinity of her heart.

She missed Tyler and what they'd shared that evening before she'd stopped the madness. Not the sexual intimacy, but the outpouring of emotion that had filled her heart. The ache for what could never be grew to startling proportions.

He'd maintained his distance, giving her the unconditional friendship she'd requested as they worked together to familiarize Roman Warrior with his new environment. On a business level, their relationship couldn't be more perfect.

He'd been great with Daniel, giving the boy his undivided attention as he taught him how to break the fillies. Daniel was gradually opening up to Tyler, accepting him with a reserved respect that clutched at Brianne's maternal instincts. Yet she found she could no longer deny Daniel the pleasure of knowing his "Uncle Tyler." It was the only discreet way she could offer both son and father the chance to know one another.

And as each day passed, telling Tyler the truth about Daniel became harder to do. For as much as she loved Tyler, and as much as she wanted to share the secret with him, she feared he'd hate her for her deception, for marrying someone as spiteful as Boyd when she'd been pregnant with *his* child, despite her reasons for doing so.

She hated Boyd for manipulating the situation to his advantage, and she hated herself for being so weak and scared that she'd allowed him to take everything away from Tyler that he'd loved. The reining operation. The ranch. Her. And the son Tyler had no knowledge of.

But her regrets changed nothing, and neither did the tears burning the back of her throat. She'd decided to make the best of the situation as it was and leave well enough alone. But the past had a way of blending with the future, and there was no forgetting the young, innocent boy who was caught in the middle of the mess she'd made of things.

The object of her thoughts entered the kitchen at that moment, a huge smile wreathing his face. His eyes sparkled with excitement beneath the youth-size chocolate-colored Stetson Tyler had purchased for him when they'd gone into town together a few days ago.

She forced a smile. "What's up, cowboy?" She playfully tugged on the brim of his Stetson, a smaller replica of the one Tyler owned, and her heart suddenly stopped.

With the hat covering his blond hair and his strikingly blue eyes staring up at her, his youthful features became more prominent, more defined. Daniel might have inherited her blond hair, but there was no denying the angle of his nose, the cut of his jaw, and the shape of his lips were his father's. The resemblance was subtle, but in a few years, as he matured from a youth, to a teenager, to a man, there'd be no mistaking the similarities between Tyler and Daniel.

She felt the floor beneath her feet dip and sway and her hand grabbed the counter for support.

Daniel frowned at her. "Mom, you okay?"

"I'm just fine," she managed, restraining the urge to confiscate his hat for fear of Tyler seeing what she had. She was being paranoid, she told herself, certain the likeness was more noticeable to her because she knew the truth.

"Where are you off to?" she asked, grabbing the spatula and removing the cookies from the pan to the cooling rack next to the oven.

"I'm going to help Uncle Tyler break a new filly." He filched a few warm cookies and bit into one. "Will you come and watch?"

She wasn't in the frame of mind to witness the closeness developing between father and son, but she couldn't avoid it, either. And she wanted to support Daniel's interest in the horses. "Maybe later, okay?"

"Okay," he said, and started out of the kitchen. He got as far as the screen door when he turned around and raced back, lifting another handful of her cookies. "Uncle Tyler likes your cookies, too," he explained, giving her an impish grin before heading out the back door.

Brianne glanced out the kitchen window, watching her son make his way down to the breaking corral and the father waiting for him. Betty was on her way up to the house, and Daniel waved to the only grandmotherly figure he'd ever known, telling her that his uncle Tyler was going to make him the second-best trainer on Whitmore Acres. Betty laughed, informed him that he made a mighty fine-looking cowboy in his new Stetson, and Daniel beamed.

Less than a minute later Betty entered the kitchen, and to Brianne's relief she didn't comment on the baked goods lining the counter. The cookies, cakes, and breads spoke for themselves. She'd always dealt with stress in the past by baking, but since Tyler's return, she no longer found the diversion therapeutic.

"It's been a long time since I've seen Daniel so happy," Betty commented with a smile. "Tyler must be the reason for the boy's new lease on life."

Brianne turned off the oven and set about pouring them each a glass of iced tea. "Yes, Tyler's been spending a lot of time with him lately."

Betty settled in at the table and accepted the glass of tea from Brianne. "The time they're spending together is good for both of them, don't you think?"

What was the other woman getting at? she wondered, trying to gauge the direction of their conversation. "As long as Daniel doesn't get hurt."

"I don't believe Tyler would ever intentionally hurt the boy, Brianne," she said, then added, "Or you."

"No, not intentionally," Brianne agreed very quietly, taking a sip of her cool drink. That much she believed. It was the unintentional part that made her nervous, when the anger and bitterness of the past collided with the present and exploded in fury. She shuddered at the thought.

After a long, quiet moment passed, Betty said, "Tyler still loves you, you know."

Shocked at the other woman's statement, she stared incredulously at her. "What in the world gave you *that* idea?"

Betty's pale blue eyes twinkled. "Why, it's obvious by the way he looks at you."

Brianne shook her head. Hard. Obvious? Was *her* love for Tyler obvious, too? "That's ridiculous," she scoffed, and began dumping the baking dishes into the soapy water in the sink.

"Not really." She shrugged, but the look in her eyes

was anything but innocent. The woman was on a mission. "Jasper told me all about that silly friendship pact of yours with Tyler, but there's more between the two of you than either of you want to admit."

"There's too much between us, Betty. That's the problem. A ranch we can't agree on, my marriage to Boyd, too much hurt..." And too many secrets.

Betty looked thoughtful. "Maybe, if you give Tyler the chance and trust him, you both can help each other heal those hurts."

How could she expect Tyler to forgive her when she couldn't even forgive herself for robbing him of so much? And if she trusted him with the truth, she'd risk his pure hatred and condemnation for what she'd done. And where would that leave Daniel?

She rubbed her temple, feeling so lost and confused. A heavy pressure settled in her chest. Feeling closed in and afraid of the unknown, she grappled for an excuse to get away.

Grabbing the truck keys off a hook next to the cupboard, she blurted the first thing that came to mind. "I've got to run to the feed store for some supplies."

Betty smiled and waved her hand in the air. "Sure, honey, you go right ahead and run along."

And as Brianne exited the kitchen to the living room, she heard Betty add, "But you can't keep running from the past, because it'll always be there until you face it."

"No doubt about it, Daniel, you're going to be a fine trainer one day," Tyler said, giving the boy's shoulder an affectionate squeeze as they left the breaking corral. They'd spent an hour together, trying to calm a filly enough to get a blanket on her back. Daniel, Tyler was learning, had a deft touch with the horses, a way of soothing their fears with just a gentle touch. "And if you'd like, I'd love to teach you about reining, too."

Daniel glanced up at him, blue eyes peering at him in a shy, hesitant way from beneath the brim of his new hat. "How come you're always so nice to me?"

Daniel's question, and the vulnerable note in his voice yanked at Tyler's heart. So many insecurities for one so young. The past week he'd spent with Daniel had shown him a gentle, sensitive side to the boy. He'd grown fond of him, and wished, not for the first time, that Daniel were his.

Dismissing the longing weaving through him, he focused on convincing the insecure boy of his self-worth. "Because I like you, and I think we can be good friends," he said simply, and honestly.

Disbelief colored Daniel's eyes to a deeper shade of blue, just before he ducked his head and scuffed his boot against the dirt drive. "Why? I'm nothin' special."

Tyler stopped at the fence bordering the pasture. Leaning his back against it and propping the heel of his boot on the bottom rung, he stared steadily at Daniel. "Sure you are."

"*Boyd* never thought so," he refuted, his tone tinged with anger and challenge.

Not Dad. *Boyd.* Daniel never had any reason to think of Boyd as a dad, and had missed out on all the fun learning experiences a father taught his son. Tyler wanted to give Daniel the masculine closeness and friendship that had been ruthlessly stolen from him.

"Boyd, your *dad,* never knew how to appreciate a good thing when he had it," he said, striving to boost Daniel's sagging morale. "You're a good, smart kid, and *very* special. Don't let anyone tell you differently."

Daniel looked at him for a long moment, as if gauging his sincerity and wanting to believe his words. The gradual trust shifting across Daniel's expression made Tyler optimistic about the future.

Before Tyler could take their conversation any further, a Ford truck ambled up the drive. Tyler recognized the driver as Larry Henshaw, a nearby rancher interested in Roman Warrior's stud services. As soon as the truck came to a stop, Jimmy, Larry's nine-year-old son and a friend of Daniel's, scrambled out of the cab and ran toward Daniel. Within minutes, the two were off and playing, leaving Tyler to conduct business with Larry uninterrupted.

Nearly an hour and a half later, Tyler shook the other man's hand, having garnered a verbal agreement for Roman Warrior's stud services to Gypsy, one of Larry's quarter horse mares.

"I'll get with Brianne and have a contract drawn up within the week for Roman's services," Tyler said as they walked from the breeding shed where Larry had examined Roman Warrior, to the main stables. Tyler glanced toward the house, searching for Brianne's truck, but noticed it was still gone. He'd expected her to be here for Larry's appointment, but she'd either forgotten, or something else had come up. "And as soon as you make a deposit, we can put Gypsy on the schedule."

"Great," Larry said enthusiastically and gave his leather hat a habitual tug. "It's a pleasure doing business with you, Tyler. Your daddy was a good man 'round these parts, and Brianne has done well with the cutting business, but it's nice to see Whitmore Acres expanding again."

"Thanks," Tyler said, though he was certain Brianne wouldn't have been pleased to hear other people were supporting his *frivolous* ideas. "I'm hoping within a few years we'll have a good solid reining operation running."

Larry grinned. "That's good to hear, and I'll be sure to spread the word."

Inside the stables, Tyler spotted Daniel alone, searching the stalls. "Where's your friend?" he asked.

"I don't know," Daniel said, his brow creased in concentration as he peered around corners and stacks of bales of hay. "We're playing hide-and-seek and I haven't been able to find him."

"Come on, son," Larry called. "We've got to get going. Your mother is going to have supper on the table and our hides skinned if we're late."

Tyler chuckled. "Can't have that, now can we?"

Larry rolled his eyes. "You know how women can be."

"Too well," he agreed, unable to understand Brianne's behavior of late.

Larry glanced at his watch and cringed. "I told her I'd be home half an hour ago. Do you mind if I give her a call just to let her know we're on our way?"

Tyler grinned and pointed to the back of the stable. "You can use the phone in the tack room."

Larry headed in that direction, and Tyler started out of the stables when a rustling sound from up in the loft caught both Daniel's and his attention.

"There he is!" Daniel squealed, and scrambled up the rickety stairs leading to the second-story platform, nearly losing his balance in his haste.

Tyler froze, staring up at the loft where Daniel had disappeared, unable to stop one unforgettable memory from replaying in his mind. He'd been twelve and had gone up to the loft to play with his army men. Boyd had found him there. After kicking his miniature army camp in ten different directions, Boyd had informed him the loft was off limits. They'd fought, and during their scuffle Boyd had maneuvered him closer to the edge, then deliberately shoved him off.

Tyler's body jerked and his stomach pitched at the vivid recollection. He could still see in his mind's eye as he'd fallen backward, his hands helplessly grappling the empty air…and Boyd's malicious smile as he'd watched him plummet to the ground.

He'd ended up with a broken arm and a concussion. Fearing further retribution from Boyd for "snitching," he'd told Landon he'd slipped and fallen. Since that day, he'd never been up in a loft.

And he didn't like that Daniel and Jimmy were up there unchaperoned, either. "Hey, guys, I don't think you should be up there."

Daniel stopped at the end of the platform and glanced down. "Why not?"

Tyler jammed his hands on his hips. "Because it's not safe."

Daniel dismissed him with a wave of a hand and walked out of sight. "I come up here all the time. Jasper cleaned it out for me. It's kinda like a tree house, but without the tree."

"It's really cool up here," Jimmy said. He skipped to the edge and came to a skidding halt that had him teetering for balance.

Tyler's heart slammed in his chest, and he automatically positioned himself below where the boy stood. "Get away from the edge," he said, his voice harsher than he'd intended. He dragged in a deep breath, and attempted to reason with them more calmly. "It's getting late and Jimmy has to go home. I think you both should come down."

"But it's fun up here, Uncle Tyler," Daniel said from somewhere Tyler couldn't see. "I've got a neat telescope set up by the window. Wanna see it? Maybe you can come up here later when it gets dark and we can look at the skinny dipper together.''

"Maybe another night," he said impatiently. He heard thumping on the floorboards as one of them ran from one end of the loft to the other. "Daniel and Jimmy, would you stop running around up there. You guys are going to end up hurting yourself. In fact, I'd appreciate it if you came down," he requested for the third time.

"Aw, come on, Uncle Tyler—"

"Get your butts down here, *now!*" he said through clenched teeth.

"Betcha can't catch me," Daniel taunted his friend in a typical boyish way, ignoring Tyler's demand.

"Bet I can!"

Horrified, Tyler listened as the boys chased each other, both of them growling and laughing. They came precariously close to the edge, oblivious to the danger, then sprinted out of sight again.

"Hey!" he bellowed, just as a loud crack rent the air, along with a cry of alarm. The next instant a "thump" echoed in the stable, and Tyler instinctively knew one of the boys had fallen.

"Daniel!" Jimmy cried, the sound ripping through Tyler like a dozen knives.

"Damn," he cursed, and without hesitating he grasped the rungs on the ladder, leaving his childhood fear behind. He spotted Daniel first, sitting on the floor, looking dazed but unharmed. His foot had smashed through the first layer of the plank floor. Jimmy squatted next to him, his eyes wide as he watched Tyler approach.

"I'm sorry, Mr. Whitmore," Jimmy said, swallowing nervously. "We were just having a little fun."

Relief at finding them safe took some of the edge off his anger. "What happened?"

"The floorboard was loose and my shoe got caught,"

Daniel said, reaching to pull the splintered board away from his foot.

Kneeling beside him, Tyler brushed the boy's hands away so he could assess the situation. "Are you okay?"

"Yeah, it just scared me," he said sheepishly.

"And you scared the hell out of me." Tyler shot him a grim look and removed the loose flooring.

"Sorry," Daniel murmured, lifting his undamaged foot out of the shallow hole.

Tyler's stern gaze encompassed them both. "If you guys would have listened to me in the first place and came down when I asked you to, this never would have happened—"

"Hey, how did that old box get in there?" Daniel asked abruptly.

Tyler frowned at the interruption in his lecture, and glanced back at the hole in the floor. He stared in shock at the handmade wooden box he'd crafted in wood shop when he'd been in junior high. He'd made the box for Father's Day for Landon, but the day before the big event, the box had mysteriously disappeared.

He'd always suspected Boyd of stealing the gift, but like everything else, he'd had no proof. And Boyd had hid the box in the one place Tyler was sure never to trespass again.

"Wow," Jimmy breathed, looking at Tyler in awe. "Just like a secret treasure."

Tyler wondered exactly what kind of treasures the box held.

"Let's see what's in it," Daniel said as if reading his thoughts. Withdrawing the box, he lifted the lid. "Look at all this neat stuff." Excitement laced his voice.

Stunned by the contents, Tyler sat back on his heels while Daniel revealed fragments of his childhood: his lucky rabbit's foot, his favorite G.I. Joe action figure, a quarter horse patch he'd won at his first junior cutting competition, and other personal possessions he'd thought he'd lost or misplaced. To any one else the items would be inconsequential, but to him each object had been special in some way.

"There's even a picture of Mom in here," Daniel said, taking out a wallet-size photograph.

Jimmy glanced over Daniel's shoulder as he fingered what had once been Tyler's lucky cat-eyed marble. "She sure was pretty."

Tyler cleared the knot of emotion from his throat. "Let me see that."

Daniel shrugged, handed over the picture, then continued rummaging through the box.

Tyler recognized the snapshot as Brianne's senior class picture, the one she'd given him shortly after they'd started dating. He'd carried it in his wallet, until one day his wallet turned up missing. He'd thought one of the hands had lifted it, or it had fallen out of his pocket while he'd been riding. The truth burned through him like acid.

His wallet wasn't in the box, just Brianne's picture, her image slightly faded from handling. How long did Boyd have his sights set on Brianne? Tyler wondered. Had Boyd coveted *everything* he'd treasured?

"Hey, Uncle Tyler." Daniel frowned in confusion as he handed him an envelope. "Here's an old letter addressed to you. It's from Grandpa Landon. I wonder who put it up here."

Tyler knew who the culprit was, but kept the answer to himself, unwilling to explain the extent of Boyd's hatred to Boyd's own son. Insides twisting, he retrieved the missive that had already been torn open.

The envelope was addressed to him, at one of the many ranches he'd worked on for a short time before drifting to another spread. Left No Forwarding Address, Return To Sender, was stamped in bold letters across the front. He registered the date below those words, and realized the letter had returned before Landon died.

Boyd had intercepted the letter, Tyler realized, leaving Landon to believe he'd ignored his attempt to find him. Guilt assailed him, along with a healthy dose of anger at Boyd's treachery.

"Aren't you going to read it?" Daniel asked.

He dragged his fingers through his hair, hesitation and hope warring within him. After a few moments' consideration, he pulled the letter from the envelope. Jimmy and Daniel's voices receded and his heartbeat accelerated as he read the correspondence addressed to him seven years ago.

Dear Tyler,

I'd always hoped you'd come back home on your own, but now I realize I might not get the chance to see you again. I have cancer, and Dr. Owens has given me only a few months to live.

Two years have passed since you left Whitmore Acres, and there isn't a day that goes by that I don't think about you, and hope you are happy. I regret shutting down the reining operation, and taking away the one thing you'd worked so hard for. My decision had been rash, based solely on the poor financial figures Boyd showed me. Boyd was managing the ranch, and I trusted his judgment, never believing his intentions were to deliberately drive you away.

Boyd has changed drastically since you left. He shows no interest in the horses, or the land, and I fear he will run the ranch into bankruptcy. I am too weak to run the operation myself. That's why it's so important to me that you return to reclaim what is rightfully yours. Whitmore Acres is a part of you, and regardless of your parentage, you, too, have always been a part of me.

Don't judge Brianne too harshly for the decisions she's made. We all have to make choices we aren't necessarily happy with, or proud of. She's helping me through my illness, and little Daniel has brought me much joy. Even at a year, he's already showing a love for the horses, and a fascination with the ranch. With the proper guidance he'll learn to appreciate what will one day belong to him.

Son, I await your homecoming, and I pray you return soon. Whitmore Acres needs you to continue to grow and flourish. If I don't make it before you return, don't grieve for my passing, but remember me with fond memories, as the man who loved you and taught you about horses and the land. Take your inheritance and make Whitmore Acres something to be proud of, a legacy to pass on to your children as I've passed it on to you. My greatest hope is that the ranch will remain in the family for generations to come.

Love,
Landon

The words on the paper blurred as a stinging moisture filled Tyler's eyes. An overwhelming pressure squeezed his chest. Landon *had* tried to locate him, even though he'd given him no reason to want to. He'd allowed a bitter argument instigated by Boyd to drive a wedge between him and Landon, instead of fighting Boyd's accusations about the reining operation failing. He'd let his resentment fester until coming home was no longer an option, but a mission he dreaded. It had been easier to stay away than to face Brianne's betrayal, Boyd's deceit, and Landon's disappointment.

An odd mixture of relief and anguish churned within him as he read through the letter again. He berated himself for being so selfish at the same time he absorbed the comfort Landon offered through his letter. Despite all his faults and weaknesses, Landon had found it within his heart to forgive him.

Now it was time to forgive himself.

Brianne found Tyler down by the east pasture watching the horses graze. His forearms were braced on the top rung of the fencing, his hip cocked to accommodate the old scuffed leather boot propped on the bottom rung. Faded denim molded to his lean and muscular frame, and she caught his profile as he turned his head and tilted back his Stetson.

He seemed deep in thought, and she couldn't help but wonder what was going through his mind. She came up beside him, but he didn't glance her way.

"I thought you were going to be here for Larry's appointment so we could discuss the terms of Roman Warrior's services together," he said, his voice low and sandpaper-rough as he focused his gaze on something out in the pasture.

"I forgot," she said, hating to admit that truth. She'd been so wrapped up in the turmoil and confusion from her afternoon talk with Betty, that she'd let business slide. That wasn't a good sign, and she'd be sure not to let her emotions rule her head again.

"We've got our first paid-for mare for Roman Warrior and plenty more interested prospects," he told her.

She settled her arms on the fencing, wondering if he ever planned to look her way. Was he that upset with her for missing the appointment? "That's good to hear."

Finally, he turned his head and glanced at her. His mouth lifted in a slight smile, but there was something in his expression that made her own reciprocating smile stop before it formed. He looked different suddenly, older and ragged around the edges. Deep in his eyes revealed an ancient pain that tugged at her.

Wanting to offer the comfort he seemed to need, even if it was only a physical touch, she laid her hand on his arm. "Tyler, what is it?"

Without a word, he withdrew an envelope from his back pocket. She had the fleeting thought that he'd received a letter that would take him away from Whitmore Acres. Mixed emotions filtered through her, and a painful lump formed in her chest.

"Did you get some bad news?" she asked, surprised her vocal cords still functioned. Leaning forward, she tried to see who the letter was addressed to and who the sender was, but he held the correspondence at such an angle she couldn't read the front.

"Not exactly." Running his finger over the edge of the envelope, he looked back up at her, his gaze shadowed. "Down in the stables, Daniel and I found a box I'd made in wood shop. The box was stashed in the loft."

"Oh." What did a box have to do with the envelope in his hand?

Tyler explained how Boyd must have hidden the wooden box there, and about Daniel getting his foot caught in the floorboard, which lead to the discovery. "The box was filled with a bunch of my stuff I'd thought I'd lost."

"You mean Boyd stole your things?" she asked incredulously.

"It appears that way. I found this letter addressed to me," he said, finally revealing the front of the envelope and the attempt that had been made to deliver the correspondence. "It was from Landon, but I never received it, and Boyd obviously intercepted the returned letter so Landon would think I ignored his attempt to find me.''

"What did Landon say in the letter?''

He held her gaze for what seemed like an eternity, then handed her the unfolded letter. ''Why don't you read it for yourself?'' he said quietly.

Taking the letter, she read the heartfelt correspondence. By the time she'd finished, tears of happiness brimmed in her eyes. ''I told you Landon loved you.''

He smiled, the doubts and self-recriminations gone from his eyes. Very gently, he wiped away the trail of tears on her cheek with his thumb. ''Yes, you did.''

Unable to help herself, she pressed her cheek into his warm palm, reveling in this brief moment of closeness between them. ''Now do you believe it?''

''I think a part of me always believed he loved and forgave me for leaving the way I did,'' he said. ''I've just been too caught up in my own guilt to admit it.'' Taking the letter back, he put it in the envelope. ''Where did you bury him?''

''You know how much he loved this land. Before he died he asked to be buried here. There's a plot out in the west meadow.''

He pulled in a deep breath and let it rush out, as if purging himself of any old, lingering demons. Then his clear and bright gaze captured hers. ''I've got Roman Warrior scheduled to breed with Sweet Justice in the morning. Will you take me to Landon tomorrow afternoon?''

''Yes, if that's what you want.''

''It is.'' He stared at the envelope in his hand. A sense of serenity drifted across his features when he glanced back at her. ''I think it's time to tell my father goodbye.''

*   *   *

The following afternoon Brianne and Tyler were mounted on horses and on their way to Landon's gravesite, the leather saddles creaking as the horses swayed lazily beneath them. The day was warm, the sky an endless stretch of blue as they strolled into a green pasture with a forest of trees banking either side.

Tyler thumbed his hat back and slid his gaze to her. The sun cast a sparkling gold hue to his blue eyes, making him appear young and happy. "If all goes well, next summer we should have ourselves our first foal from Roman Warrior."

Brianne didn't want to think or plan that far ahead into the future. Not when the present seemed so unstable and uncertain. "We've already generated some interest from the ad we placed for stud services. Two of my cutting clients want to purchase pleasure horses and another wants to breed one of his mares to Roman Warrior."

A wholly masculine grin spread across his face. "Sounds like Roman Warrior is going to be busy the next few months. Didn't I tell you he'd be a solid investment?"

"Yes, you did," she conceded, running her fingers along Cameo's soft neck.

"Then maybe you'll be able to trust me a bit more."

Brianne heard the underlying question and hope in his words, and knew he was referring to more than just the ranch and business decisions. He wanted her complete trust, personally and emotionally, yet that was the one thing she couldn't bring herself to give him, no matter how much her heart yearned to.

It was difficult living with him, talking with him, and wanting him the way she did. But as always when she experienced that deep pang of longing, she reminded herself of the risk of letting down her guard and loving

Tyler so completely. Daniel had accepted him as Uncle Tyler, and for now, that's all she could allow him to be. A friend. Anything more would complicate their business relationship.

"Which way?" Tyler asked, bringing her back to the present and the twin trails leading in opposite directions.

"Over here." She guided Cameo in front of the horse Tyler rode and veered off from the open pasture.

Tyler followed Brianne down a grassy trail that led them through a cool shaded forest of trees. Wildflowers bloomed all around them, and he breathed deeply of the scents of damp earth, fresh grass and cool, clear water.

Brianne brought Cameo to a halt, and Tyler stopped beside her, taking in the lush beauty and babbling brook in front of them. Clear water rushed over smooth rocks, the sound soothing and oddly calming.

"His marker is just over that knoll," Brianne said quietly.

A flutter of nerves hatched within him. Suddenly, he felt like a kid facing a momentous task. "Will you come with me?" he asked.

She smiled, as if understanding his apprehension. "If you want me to."

"I do."

He dismounted, then reached up and clasped her waist to help her down before he tethered the horses to a low tree limb so they could graze. No words were exchanged as hand in hand, Brianne led Tyler alongside the brook to a clearing in the meadow. More wildflowers blossomed everywhere upon the soft, high-grade soil, their stems swaying in the light breeze.

And then he saw the marble marker, just beneath a huge shady tree. Untangling his fingers from Brianne's, he walked slowly toward the headstone and knelt before it, a knot of emotion forming in his chest. He read the epitaph, traced the words and numbers with his finger. A swell of tears burned the backs of his eyes.

Plucking at a stray weed, he threw it aside and reached for another. There was so much he wanted to say to Landon, but mere words and thoughts eluded him at the moment. Then, as if Landon were there with him and knew what troubled him, the guilt and agony and regret of the past nine years flowed from him in a breathtaking rush of feeling. And when it was over, a lightness settled over him, wiping out the loneliness and solitude that had filled his soul for so long.

He sat there for what could have been minutes or hours, silently communicating his thoughts and feelings to Landon and knowing in his heart his father heard him. He remembered all the good times he'd shared with Landon, and made peace with himself.

He unchained the past, letting go of all the bitterness and resentment he'd carried for too long. Whispering a final farewell to the man he'd called Dad, Tyler stretched to his full height and faced Brianne. She sat on a cluster of rocks by the brook, too far away for his liking, giving him the privacy he'd needed moments ago, but no longer wanted.

He approached her, and she slid off the rock and stood, watching him warily.

He gathered her in his arms, smiling at her startled intake of breath. She stiffened, and he embraced her tighter, until she finally relaxed and wrapped her arms around his waist to hug him back.

"Tyler?"

He buried his face in the soft, fragrant hair she'd left unbound, never wanting to let her go. "Oh, God, Brianne. It feels so good. I feel so free and peaceful inside."

"I'm glad," she whispered against his ear, but there

was a trace of uncertainty in her voice that tugged at him.

He pulled back and threaded his fingers through her hair. Tilting her head back, he gazed deeply into her eyes. "Everything is going to be just fine," he told her, wondering who he was trying to convince. Then he lowered his mouth and kissed her, because it seemed so right.

The kiss was sweet, a rejoicing of spirit and soul. A promise of the future, of planting new, binding roots of love and commitment, and watching them grow.

If only she'd put aside her own securities and reach out and take what he so freely offered.

CHAPTER TEN

"NICE of you to donate all these cakes and cookies for the refreshment table, Brianne."

Brianne smiled at her friend, Emily Harper, the young, energetic woman responsible for organizing the annual dance social, which was held in Emily's husband's huge, renovated barn.

"I was happy to help," she said, arranging a plate of maple walnut bars among the abundance of goodies covering the table.

Emily selected a fudge caramel brownie from a tray as she swayed to an upbeat country tune the hired D.J. played. "Well, you certainly made enough to feed the entire town."

"She's been baking all week just for the occasion," Tyler drawled, sidling next to Brianne and filching a few peanut butter cookies for himself. "Haven't you, Bree?"

"I always bake for the annual dance," she replied, casting him a go-away-you're-bothering-me look.

He winked at her, the playful charm he'd exuded the past week still going strong. Shaking her head at his behavior, she glanced at the crowd of people having a good time, two-stepping and kicking up sawdust in the middle of the barn's hardwood floor.

Emily's husband claimed his wife to join the mob of people starting a line dance, and Al Thayer, an old family friend of the Whitmores, came by and whisked Tyler away to reunite with a group of men gathered by the beer keg near the service bar, leaving Brianne to supervise the refreshment table alone.

Ladling punch into a Styrofoam cup, she handed it to the little boy standing on the other side of the table. From across the room she watched Tyler shake hands and endure hearty slaps on the back as friends welcomed him home. She couldn't help but notice how everyone accepted Tyler as one of their own, as if he'd only been gone a few short weeks instead of nine long years.

She spent the next half hour visiting with friends as they stopped by the refreshment table, and handing out goodies to the kids. Glancing around the barn for Daniel, she found him standing next to Tyler within the cluster of men. Tyler had his arm slung affectionately over Daniel's shoulder, including him in the conversation. The two had grown close over the weeks, and Brianne experienced a brief stab of guilt for the secret she still hid from Tyler, and for denying her son the opportunity to know his real father. The feelings of deceit occurred more and more often lately, making her question if she was doing the right thing by withholding the truth.

After a while Tyler made his way back to her. "How about a dance?" he asked, flashing that charming grin of his.

"Where's Daniel?" she asked, ignoring his question and the way her heart beat faster at the thought of being held in Tyler's arms.

"He's with Betty," he replied, handing six-year-old Eddie Williams the chocolate cupcake he stared at longingly. "She said she'd look after him so we could enjoy our date."

She rolled her eyes at his presumptuousness. "This isn't a date."

He frowned at her, but there was a twinkle in his eyes that put her on alert. "No?"

"No," she stated resolutely, smiling at her postman, Harold Evans, as he sampled a piece of her fudge.

Obviously finding it to his liking, he lifted two more squares and headed back to the dance floor to join his wife and the ten-step in progress. "If I remember correctly, you invited yourself along."

Instead of looking contrite, a cocky grin curved his mouth. "You wanted me to come."

"I said no such thing."

Tyler gently grasped the hand reaching for a plate of Rice Krispies treats and drew her away from the bustle around the refreshment table to a semiprivate area a few feet away. Leaning close, he touched his finger to her mouth, rubbing her full bottom lip with a mesmerizing slowness.

"It wasn't your mouth that was talking, darlin'," he drawled in a low, intimate voice. "It was your eyes. Trust me, they invited me to the dance."

A snappy comeback eluded her. Her senses were under siege, bombarded by the warm, male scent of him. She tried to take a safe step back, but there was nowhere to go. She realized, belatedly, that he'd trapped her between his body and the wall. With his hand braced by the side of her head, his large, muscular body cast her in shadow, cocooning them from the rest of the guests. The music, people, and general noise faded away.

"Besides," he continued with a lazy shrug that somehow shifted his lower body closer so his thighs brushed hers, causing an electrical current of heat to ripple through her. "How would it have looked if I'd let you come to the dance unescorted?"

Her spine stiffened against rough wood. "I'm a big girl, Tyler, and very capable of taking care of myself."

"I know you are. If there's one thing I've learned in the past couple of weeks, it's that you're one fiercely independent woman. I wouldn't dare try to change that," he said, his fingers fluttering along her jaw in a butterfly caress. "The truth is, I wanted to come tonight because I have this fantasy about slow dancing with you. Do you realize we've never slow danced before?"

No, they'd never slow danced before. The mere thought of her body pressing so intimately against his and moving in a provocative rhythm to the music made her pulse race.

He was deliberately tempting her with his outrageous words, his subtle moves, and his eyes. Oh, Lord, his eyes had the ability to melt every lick of common sense she owned. She found herself relaxing, softening, letting down barriers better left erected. Casting him an upswept look, she gave in to the impulse to run her hand up his arm, reveling in the firm, warm muscle beneath her palm.

"Are you flirting with me, Tyler Whitmore?" she asked, surprising herself at the sultry quality of her voice.

His eyes darkened perceptively. "I'm trying my damnedest. Is it working yet?"

She smiled, enjoying their playful banter, as dangerous as it was to her heart. "Not yet, but you're getting close."

"Not close enough," he said meaningfully, smoky desire evident in his gaze. "But I'm working on it. Did I happen to mention how beautiful you look tonight?"

Her breath caught as he slowly trailed a finger down her neck and into the collar of her dress. "At least three times," she said in a soft voice.

"Oh." He frowned contemplatively and moved slightly, slipping his thigh between hers with consummate ease. "Did I happen to mention how much I like this dress on you, because it shows off your legs?"

"Only twice," she whispered, falling deeper into the spell he wove, so that she forgot where they were.

Forgetting, too, all the reasons why she should keep her distance from him.

"Oh." The creases between his brows deepened, but there was a ruthless, possessive light in his eyes more erotic than anything she'd ever encountered.

Picking up a skein of her hair, he rubbed the strands between his fingers, then slowly sank his hands into the soft waves, burying his fingers in the mass and tugging gently. "Did I happen to mention how much I love your hair down? That it reminds me of the night we almost made love and the way my fingers caught in the silky strands as I kissed you?"

Her throat tightened. A rush of awareness settled where his thigh pressed so insistently. "No," she managed to answer, though she didn't think his question required one.

"Well, now you know," he said, breathing warm air into her ear, sending tingles down her spine. "Every time I look at you I think about that night, how soft and eager you were and how close we came to making love."

"Stop," she moaned, her face warming at the passionate memories his words evoked.

"Why?" He lifted his head, his eyes blazing with a hunger more emotional than sexual. "It's the truth."

"We're in a roomful of people."

"And if we weren't, I'd be doing my damnedest to finish what we started in that motel room—"

She slapped her hand over his mouth. "You're not playing fair."

Pulling her hand away, he kissed her fingers with a reverence that made her ache. "When it comes to something I want, I never do."

She closed her eyes for a moment, succumbing to his

tantalizing seduction. "Tyler, what am I going to do with you?"

He nipped at her fingers with his teeth. "I have a few ideas, but I have to warn you, they're not very appropriate for a public place."

She shook her head regretfully. "You're incorrigible."

He stepped back, a grin quirking his mouth. "Yeah, I know."

Their gazes locked for a timeless moment, until Sheriff Jacobsen's deep voice interrupted the silent yearning and sensual promises passing between them.

"Hey, Brianne, you got any more of those great maple walnut bars left?"

Tyler sighed and caressed his thumb over her cheek. "Saved in the nick of time, wouldn't you say?" he murmured to her, his tone rueful.

Not trusting herself to speak for all the emotions flooding her senses, she nodded at Tyler. Seizing the opportunity while it presented itself, she slipped away from him and resumed her post at the refreshment table. She opened a plastic container holding extra goodies and held it toward Gary Jacobsen so he could take a few maple walnut bars.

"You're supposed to be having a good time," Tyler said from beside her once the sheriff left, frustration edging into his tone. "Not standing guard at the refreshment table all night long."

She flashed him a smile, still shaken by their arousing escapade. "What makes you think I'm not having a good time?"

He scowled at her. "You've spent the entire evening fussing over the cakes and cookies you baked. You're driving me crazy." Before she could protest, he grabbed her hand, laced their fingers tightly together, and dragged her toward the sawdusted dance floor.

"Tyler!" she said indignantly. "What do you think you're doing?"

"Showing you how to have a good time."

She had no choice but to follow him as he wove around the crowd of people leaving the dance area as the current fast song ended and a slow, romantic ballad started. In the next instant she found herself pulled into his arms, her body flushed to his. Her heart tripled its beat and warmth suffused the length of her.

Tyler cocked an ear toward the melody drifting out of the speakers mounted on the high beams above them. "Would you listen to that?" he said, his handsome face a study in seriousness.

She frowned, striving to hear the significant something he apparently heard. "What?"

His gaze fused with hers. A breathtaking smile spread across his face and grabbed at her heart. "They're playing our song."

She rolled her eyes at him. "We don't have a song, Tyler."

"We do now, darlin'," he said, his deep, husky voice filled with satisfaction.

Brianne's stomach tumbled and a lump formed in her chest as George Strait's smooth vocals wrapped around her as he sang the lyrics to "I Cross My Heart."

Someone dimmed the lights for the romantic ballad, and Tyler swept his hand slowly down her spine, aligning them intimately. His hips moved with hers, and he bent his head so his lips skimmed the sensitive flesh just below her ear. Despite all her good intentions to resist him, she flowed into him, wrapping her arms around his neck, wanting him so badly her heart hurt.

Then he sang the heartfelt lyrics to her, about sharing

love and laughter and a lifetime together, and promising to give her all he had to make her dreams come true.

Biting her lip to keep the tears at bay, she looked into his eyes and saw a glimmer of something deep and everlasting. Love filled her empty soul. Declarations and wishes whirled in her, frightening her with their strength, yet she kept them bottled up tight. In that moment, feeling his heart beat in cadence with hers, the insurmountable obstacles that had once separated them didn't seem so vast.

"Am I getting close yet?" he teased in a husky voice.

"Yes," she whispered in his ear. Closer than he realized. He was burrowed into her heart and soul, a part of her forever, no matter what happened in the future.

He smiled against her throat. "Mmm. You feel so good. You smell even better."

"Tyler," she breathed, wishing they were alone.

The slow, haunting song ended and the lights gradually brightened, leaving Brianne overwhelmed by the flood of emotions rushing through her. The look in Tyler's sapphire eyes told her all she needed to do was extend the invitation, and he was hers. The fantasy tempted her, and she felt reckless enough to live for the moment. Or for the night.

The rest of the evening was magical, full of tender looks and stolen kisses when Tyler caught her alone outside enjoying the breeze and stars overhead. By the time they arrived home, Brianne wasn't sure she could resist Tyler, or deny what they both wanted so badly...to make love.

Daniel fell asleep in the truck on the drive home, and Tyler carried him up to his room while Brianne turned down his bed. Once Daniel was settled in, she closed the door to his room and turned to face Tyler, who leaned against the wall, watching her.

Tyler recognized the soft desire in Brianne's eyes, and knew it was only a matter of leading her to the master bedroom at the end of the hall, where he could strip her naked, press her down on the bed and thoroughly love her. His body throbbed with the knowledge.

She held out her hand in silent invitation.

A deep shudder went through him. He'd waited so long for this, for *her,* but what would happen tomorrow when they had to face one another in the light of day? Would she withdraw from him emotionally again? He didn't think he could bear the rejection, not when he wanted more from her...promises, her love, and a lifetime of making love guilt-free.

Yet she'd given him no indication she wanted the same.

It was that thought that gave him the strength to refuse what she so openly offered. He needed more than a night of satisfying, forget-everything-else-in-the-world sex, and until she trusted him completely, with her heart and soul and not just her body, their relationship would remain unconsummated.

He leaned toward her, and her lips parted on a soft sigh. But instead of claiming those lips like she expected him to, like he *ached* to, he brushed a chaste kiss on her cheek and murmured, "Good night, Bree."

Thrusting his hands into his jeans' pockets to keep from touching her, he headed into the guest room and quietly closed the door, certain the confusion and hurt he'd seen shimmering in her eyes would haunt him for the rest of the night.

The next morning Tyler rose at the early hour of five-thirty to take Daniel fishing, as he'd promised the boy earlier in the week. By six-thirty they sat side by side on a grassy incline bordering a lake, alone in their private alcove. The morning sun warmed their backs and shimmered off the glasslike surface of the water.

"Thanks for taking me fishing, Uncle Tyler."

Tyler smiled at Daniel as they baited their hooks. "I can't think of a better way to spend a Sunday morning," he replied, remembering how much he'd enjoyed fishing with Landon when he'd been Daniel's age.

"Maybe we could do this *every* Sunday," Daniel suggested hopefully, casting his line into the lake. "Just the two of us."

Tyler liked the way that sounded. A lot. He couldn't believe how quickly he'd come to care for Daniel, and how much the idea of being a part of his life appealed to him. Now he only had to convince Brianne that they were meant to be a family.

"Maybe we could," Tyler said, casting his line a couple of yards from Daniel's. "But I was wondering if you'd be interested in reining lessons Sunday mornings, along with learning to break the fillies."

A subdued glimmer of expectation lit Daniel's gaze. "Reining lessons?"

"Sure." He placed his fishing pole in a bracket, then ruffled Daniel's blond head affectionately. "We can start slow and easy, and maybe by next year you'll be ready to compete in an amateur rodeo."

A bright smile wreathed Daniel's face. "You think so?"

"Absolutely." Stretching on the old blanket they'd brought along, Tyler cupped his hands at the back of his head and settled in for the inevitably long wait that came with fishing. "All it takes is hard work and lots of practice. Think you're up to it?"

Daniel nodded eagerly. "Yeah."

"Good." Tyler closed his eyes and absorbed the sun's warm rays, feeling content and lazy and very optimistic.

"I caught a fish!"

Daniel's shout startled Tyler out of his peacefulness. He blinked his eyes open. "What?"

"I caught a fish," Daniel repeated excitedly, his eyes as big as saucers. He pulled with all his might as the tip of his pole bowed toward the lake. "Uncle Tyler, help! It's a big one!"

Tyler jumped to his feet and together they worked to reel in the impressive-size fish. Companionable laughter filled the air as they tried to still the foot-long trout flopping on the shore so they could remove the hook from its mouth.

"This is so cool," Daniel said in awe a while later as they sat drinking a soda and admiring his catch. "Boyd and I never did stuff like this."

Not for the first time, the informal reference made Tyler pause. "You mean your *dad*."

Daniel crushed the empty Coke can in his hand, then pitched it into the cooler. He glanced at Tyler, his expression holding shadows of old pain. "Nah, he wasn't my dad," he said quietly.

Daniel's confession momentarily stunned Tyler, until he realized the boy probably meant that Boyd hadn't acted like a dad to him. "Of course he was your dad," Tyler said, trying to smooth out the awkward moment. "I know he didn't treat you the best, but he's still the man who fathered you."

"He wasn't my dad," Daniel repeated adamantly, his spine straightening. Rebellion turned his gaze a stormy shade of blue. "And I'm glad he's not my dad. He was mean to me and Mom and I didn't like him."

Tyler stared at Daniel, a sense of unease prickling just beneath the surface of his skin. He found himself searching Daniel's face, looking for some reflection of himself. But all he saw was Brianne's fair complexion and hair, and indistinguishable features set in a boyish face. He shook his head at the ridiculous thoughts running through his head. Daniel couldn't be his... Maybe Daniel had gotten his facts mixed up somehow, or just *wished* Boyd wasn't his dad.

"What makes you think Boyd's not your dad?" he asked with forced casualness, trying to dismiss the emotions playing tug-of-war within him. When Daniel hesitated, Tyler prompted him. "Did Boyd tell you he's not your dad?"

Daniel picked up a smooth rock and pitched it into the lake, not looking at him. "No," he finally said. "I heard Boyd yelling at Mom one night. I got out of bed and stood outside their bedroom door because I was afraid Boyd was going to hurt Mom. They didn't know I was listening."

Anticipation and dread churned in his belly. "What did you hear?"

He glanced at Tyler, his gaze brimming with too much hurt. Tyler almost told Daniel it didn't matter what had been said that fateful night between Boyd and Brianne. Almost. Sensing the importance of Daniel's answer, he pressed forward. "What did Boyd say?"

Sadness passed over Daniel's features, and in a barely audible voice he said, "Boyd told Mom that I'd never be anything more than the bastard my real dad was."

Tyler's heart stopped beating. A crushing heaviness settled in his chest like a hundred-pound weight. He was dimly aware of the high-pitched ringing in his ears. *You're a bastard, Tyler.* Boyd's cruel taunts of his parentage filtered through his mind, giving Daniel's admission a startling clarity of meaning.

Oh, God.

"Do you know who your real dad is?" His voice

sounded odd to his ears, tortured even, matching the ra-
zor sharpness ripping through his soul.

"No." Daniel shrugged and tossed another stone into
the lake, oblivious to Tyler's turmoil. "But it doesn't
matter."

But it *did* matter, Tyler thought in silent anguish.
Because *he* was Daniel's dad, and he should have been
there for him...

Conflicting emotions raged in him. Guilt. Anger. *Betrayal.*

A swell of nausea rose in his throat, nearly choking
him. The pain of Brianne's deceit tore at him, but more
profound was the overwhelming fury spreading through
him. After everything they'd endured in the past weeks,
she didn't trust him enough to tell him he had a son,
that Daniel was *his* son, not Boyd's.

And it was the sudden knowledge that she had no
intention of ever telling him the truth about Daniel's
parentage that sent him over the edge.

Tyler braked to a stop by the barn and glanced at the
house, knowing he had to get his temper under control
before he confronted Brianne. He turned his gaze to the
young boy sitting beside him, his *son,* and resisted blurt-
ing out the truth. As much as he wanted to claim Daniel
as his own, he wouldn't risk the boy's fragile emotions
by shocking him with such an announcement. He had a
few things to settle with Brianne first.

"I'm sorry we had to cut our fishing trip short," he
said, hating the crestfallen look on Daniel's face. "But
there's something important I need to discuss with your
mom. Why don't you unload the fishing gear then feed
Jussie for me? I'll be back down in a while."

"Okay." Reluctantly, Daniel slid out the passenger

side of the truck and began hauling the tackle into a storeroom in the barn.

Tyler started for the house. Just as he cleared the driveway Brianne came outside and stood on the porch, smiling tentatively at him. How could she act so casual when he was so furious he wanted to strangle her for deceiving him?

Brianne watched as he cut across the lawn then jogged up the porch stairs. She gasped as he gripped her arm and firmly guided her back into the house without comment. The screen door slammed shut behind them, reverberating through her like a shot. He didn't release her until they reached the living room. When she finally looked into his face, she shivered at the dark look enveloping his features.

A flutter of apprehension went through her. "Tyler, what's wrong?"

He jammed his hands on his hips, a muscle ticking in his jaw. "You weren't going to tell me, were you?" His voice was low and even, but there was an unmistakable undercurrent of bitterness to his words.

Stark fear seized her, and she automatically retreated a step. "I don't know what you're talking about."

He walked toward her, stopping inches away. His presence suddenly intimidated her, made her want to bolt from the accusations in his gaze.

"You know damn well what I'm talking about," he said. "Answer me."

Oh, God, no, she thought in despair. But the knowledge of the secret she'd kept sacred for nine long years reflected in his eyes, along with an abundance of hurt.

He knew. Somehow, he knew.

"Where's Daniel?" she asked past the tightness in her throat, not wanting him to overhear this conversation.

"Down in the barn. I told him to stay there until I came to get him."

His gaze locked with hers, the intensity of his stare so disarming she stopped breathing. And then the explosion came.

"He's mine, isn't he?" he said, his fists clenching at his sides. "For God's sake, Brianne, for once be straight with me!"

The torment in Tyler's voice reached deep inside of her, yanking at vital emotions. She couldn't lie to him. Not anymore.

Risking everything to ease some of his grief, she offered him the truth. "Yes," she whispered.

Tyler made an anguished sound, as though he'd been mortally wounded. Stumbling to the couch, he sank into the cushions, resting his head against the back to stare at the ceiling.

"How did you find out?" she dared to ask.

He glared, his gaze granite hard. "Daniel."

"Daniel?" She frowned, sure she'd misunderstood him.

A caustic smile curved his mouth. "Yeah, he heard Boyd tell you that Daniel would never be anything more than the bastard his *real* dad is."

"Oh, no," she groaned, covering her face with her hands. Wondering what else Daniel knew, she looked back at Tyler. "Does he know you're his—"

"Don't worry," Tyler interrupted, hostility sharpening his voice. "He doesn't suspect his 'Uncle Tyler' is his real father."

What a mess, Brianne thought, dragging her hands through her hair as she paced the length of the hearth, her mind whirling toward the new set of complications awaiting her. How would Daniel react to learning Tyler was his father? And what part would Tyler play in Daniel's life… A part-time uncle or a full-time father?

The same old question nagged at her, confusing her with the implications. Would Tyler stick around for the long haul?

"You weren't going to tell me, were you?" Tyler said, bringing her around again. "You were just going to let me believe he was Boyd's son."

She wanted to deny it, but couldn't. All the reasons for refusing Tyler the opportunity to know his son suddenly seemed so paltry in comparison to his pain and anger. She'd only wanted to protect Daniel from any more hurt.

He swore and abruptly stood. "I had a right to know he was my son!" His angry words boomed in the small room.

She stiffened defensively. "You gave up your rights when you left nine years ago."

Tyler felt the lash of her words like a physical slap. "Maybe I did give up those rights nine years ago," he agreed, "but what about now? Don't I deserve the chance to know my son, and have him know me? What are you so afraid of that you couldn't tell me the truth?"

She hesitated, letting out a long breath. "Daniel went through so much with Boyd. I didn't want him to get his hopes up about having a father when I had no idea how long you planned to stick around."

"You still believe I'm eventually going to leave?" he asked incredulously.

"You don't have a great track record for sticking around," she shot back, her voice infused with a combination of heat and hurt.

The past. Always the past. Old, painful memories he couldn't compete with, and choices and decisions that would always be a wedge between them.

"I would do anything for you, Brianne," Tyler said vehemently. "And I would never intentionally hurt you or Daniel or do anything to jeopardize the stable home you've built for your son. I've shown you every way I can that you can trust me, but you choose not to accept it."

She said nothing, just stared at him, eyes filled with anguish and a hand pressed to her throat.

His jaw clenched. "I don't want to hold on to the past anymore. I want to start my future with you and Daniel. But we can't do that until you decide the risk of trusting me is worth the gain."

He stared at her for what seemed like an eternity, waiting for a response. The hope in his gaze beseeched her, but the words he wanted to hear jammed in Brianne's throat. It took all her effort just to breathe normally and not fall apart for all the confusing feelings wreaking havoc within her.

"You can't do it, can you?" he asked, his mouth slanting in a grim half-smile.

After a long, tense silence, he shook his head in resignation and disappeared upstairs, leaving Brianne standing in the quiet, empty living room, her entire body numb. When he returned a few minutes later with his duffel bag in hand, a frisson of alarm skittered through her.

"What are you doing?" she asked, though his intentions were painfully obvious.

He looked at her, a cold emptiness in his eyes. "I'm giving you what you want. I'm leaving."

A wrenching pain nearly made her double over. She wrapped her arms around her middle to hold herself together. "Where are you going?" she asked, unable to keep the desperation from her voice.

Tyler set his duffel bag on the coffee table and turned

to face her. "I'm taking Armon up on his offer," he told her.

She took two steps toward him, then halted. "Tyler, don't...leave."

The tears shimmering in her eyes increased the torment ripping Tyler apart. He held firm to his convictions. "You don't need me, Brianne, and you sure as hell don't trust me. Other than a son who has no idea who his real father is, you've given me no reason to want to stay."

A choked sound escaped her. "What about Daniel?"

Tyler wasn't sure what she meant, but reassured her on all angles. "Don't worry, I won't tell him the truth. I'll leave that up to you, Brianne. I'll be his 'Uncle Tyler' for as long as you seem to believe it's necessary. Maybe someday, when you feel you're ready to deal with the truth and the past, you can tell him who his real father is. I don't want to hurt him, either, and right now, my staying would only hurt all of us."

And then he picked up his duffel bag and headed for the door, steeling himself against the sob he heard break from her throat.

Two hours later Brianne stood with Daniel down by the barn, watching as Tyler loaded Sweet Justice into the trailer. She couldn't believe it had come to this, couldn't believe Tyler was leaving her. Again. And this time, the agony of losing him cut across her heart like a blade.

Daniel stood beside her, watching the father he didn't even realize was his own, his eyes filled with confusion and grief. His stance was tense, defensive almost. She wanted to touch him and offer whatever solace she could, but wasn't sure if her son would welcome the tenderness from her right now.

Tyler locked up the trailer doors, and Brianne realized he hadn't taken Roman Warrior. He approached both of them, his bleak gaze flickering from Daniel, and finally to her.

She drew a deep breath, but it did nothing to ease the tightness in her chest. "What about Roman Warrior?" she managed to ask.

"He's yours, Brianne," he said, his gaze searching her face, as if putting it to memory. "I'm sure Sweet Justice is carrying his offspring. It's all I want."

A rush of helplessness cascaded over her, and before she could stop the words, she blurted, "I can't do this on my own."

A slight smile curved his mouth, but did nothing to soften the torment in his gaze. "You managed for three years on your own. You brought this ranch back to life on your own. You'll be fine."

Then Tyler approached Daniel, detesting the boy's guarded expression, especially after he'd worked so hard to break through all Daniel's shields.

"Did I do something to make you upset?" Daniel asked, his gaze shadowed.

Another lance of pain tore through Tyler. He suspected the heartache wouldn't end anytime soon. "No," he answered. How could he make Daniel understand his motives for leaving without hurting the boy any more than he already was?

A frown furrowed Daniel's brow, emphasizing the confusion in his eyes. "Then why are you leaving?"

Tyler's gaze strayed to Brianne, and he revised the real truth for his son's sake. "There's a man in Oregon who needs a trainer. I'm going to work for him."

"But what about us?" Daniel demanded, a desperate catch to his voice. "We need you, too!" Before Tyler could respond to that anguished question, Daniel went on, "And what about the Cheney rodeo? You were going to help me with my reining lessons!"

"Jasper will help you train," he said, his voice strained with a multitude of emotions he couldn't conceal.

Tears flooded Daniel's eyes, and his chin trembled. "It's not the same!"

No, Tyler thought, it wasn't the same.

Stepping closer to Daniel, he started to take his shoulders to offer him comfort, but the fear of his son rejecting the bit of tenderness stopped him from completing the action.

Instead, he ruffled his fingers through Daniel's hair, absorbing the warmth and softness of the strands. "Take care of your mother for me, okay, sport?"

Daniel swiped at the tears that had spilled down his cheek and lifted his head, trying to be brave. "I will," he said in a quivering voice.

"I love you, Daniel," Tyler said, his voice as ragged and torn as his soul.

The sun sparkled off the new batch of tears filling Daniel's eyes. "I...I love you, too, Uncle Tyler!" He threw himself into Tyler's arms, almost knocking him over with the force.

Tyler closed his eyes and hugged Daniel, memorizing his scent, the feel of his thin body that would grow into the maturity of a teenager, then a man. He didn't want to let Daniel go. He didn't want to leave. The tears he'd held at bay surged forward, burning, then seeped out his closed eyes. Damn, was he making the right choice?

He opened his eyes and met Brianne's gaze, bright with the same misery that pounded throughout his body. At least he wasn't alone in his suffering.

Finally, he released Daniel. Affectionately tousling the boy's hair one last time, he said a last goodbye. Without another word to Brianne, because there was nothing left to say, he climbed into his truck and drove away with Sweet Justice.

CHAPTER ELEVEN

WHAT had he done?

For two long, lonely weeks Tyler contemplated that question, and he always came to the same conclusion. He'd given up and left Whitmore Acres again, proving Brianne couldn't trust him.

The truth was tough to swallow.

Tyler gave Sweet Justice a gentle nudge with his booted foot, and the horse followed his lead, accepting the slow, lazy pace as they followed a gently flowing creek on Armon's property. Tipping back his hat, he gazed at the stretch of fertile land before them and automatically thought of Whitmore Acres.

Home. He wanted to go home. There was an emptiness inside him that grew with each passing day, one that only Whitmore Acres could fill. He missed Brianne, and Daniel. And the freedom and contentment the ranch had offered him.

But would Brianne welcome him home after the furious, abrupt way he'd left?

Yes, he'd been angry with her for not telling him the truth about Daniel, but now that he had time to think about her actions, he understood them for the protective instincts they were. Survival tactics honed by years of Boyd's cruelty. She'd wanted to keep Daniel safe from emotional harm, as she'd learned to do during her marriage to his half-brother.

There was no doubt in his mind that she'd married Boyd because she'd been pregnant with Daniel when he'd left, not for the ranch like he'd originally believed.

Her only greed stemmed from giving her son, *their* son, a better way of life than what she'd had. And he could hardly blame her for those motives.

Imagining her alone and frightened at eighteen wasn't difficult to do, or envisioning Boyd taking advantage of that vulnerability. And it was his own fault she'd married Boyd. He'd been undependable nine years ago, and with this latest stunt of his he'd only validated every one of Brianne's fears, that she couldn't depend on him for the long haul.

He loved her, and hadn't told her. He'd wanted her trust, but how could he expect her to give him something so elemental when he hadn't given her the best reason of all to extend that trust? And he did love her, with all his heart. A heart that was empty and aching without her. He wanted the three of them to be a family, like it should have been so long ago.

The thought made him spur Sweet Justice forward, toward Armon's ranch. He was going back to Whitmore Acres. Back to his heritage, to fight for what belonged to him. Back to where his love belonged.

For the first time in two weeks he smiled, though he knew going home and facing Brianne wouldn't be easy. But it was time for him to stop running and to face their problem of trust head-on. Believing in one another was a two-way street, a partnership of give and take...and there was only one thing he could do to offer Brianne the best reason of all to trust him.

Marry the stubborn woman.

Brianne couldn't concentrate on the contracts for Roman Warrior's services she needed to peruse and sign. Instead, her mind was consumed with thoughts of Tyler, the way he left, and most of all, the way she'd pushed him back out of her life.

Two weeks had passed since he'd packed up Sweet Justice and drove off the ranch. Not a day went by that she didn't think about him, cry over him, and wonder if the sorrow of losing him again would haunt her for the rest of her life.

He'd called for Daniel a few times and was always polite but curt to her, saying no more than the few words it took to request his son. It hurt, but what had she expected when she'd been the one to drive him away?

Blinking back a hot rush of tears, she pushed away from her desk and went to her office window, her heart feeling as heavy and sluggish as her footsteps.

For a long time she stood there, watching Daniel with Jasper as they worked on his reining lessons. Daniel was a lot like his father in the saddle, she thought, a small smile managing to break through her gloom. Agile and fluid, he moved with a natural grace that belied the power of the horse beneath him. He was fiercely dedicated, and just as determined to be the best rider his "Uncle Tyler" had ever seen.

Brianne knew he'd succeed. She'd expected him to withdraw after Tyler's departure, but instead he'd immediately started his lessons with vivacity and a driving purpose that amazed her. His ambition also brought on a bout of motherly concern. Everything Daniel did these days was motivated with the hope that his uncle Tyler would return to the ranch. What would her son do if he knew she was the one keeping Tyler away?

Even Jasper had developed an attitude, sulking around as though he'd lost his best friend. He never failed to remind her how much help Tyler had been around the ranch, and what an exceptional trainer they'd lost. Even her clients were telling her how much they'd enjoyed Tyler's professionalism and knowledge of their stock, and his ease and gentleness in breaking the horses. More times than she'd care to recall she'd been told "it was a shame she had to lose such a fine partner and trainer," followed up with "was there any chance of Tyler returning?"

Sighing wearily, she leaned her forehead against the cool windowpane, wishing the crushing despair weighing her spirits down would dissipate.

A broken laugh left her. "You brought this all on yourself, Brianne," she said to herself, her voice catching on a fresh swell of tears. "All because you were terrified of depending on Tyler." *Terrified of trusting him again. Terrified of him leaving again. Terrified of being hurt again.*

Yet her worst fears had been realized, and she had no one to blame but herself. She'd continually pushed him away so she wouldn't get hurt, and now here she was, hurting anyway. The pain went soul-deep, filling her with a hopelessness she couldn't escape. She missed Tyler. Terribly. Missed his laughter, his teasing, even their arguments.

Would the tears and misery ever end?

Taking a steadying breath before another onslaught of emotion pulled her under, she glanced around her office, absorbing the changes she'd made over the past three years. She had everything a woman could possibly want. A handsome, smart son, a nice home, and a thriving business that had the potential to grow as large as she wanted it to. She'd worked hard on this ranch, had labored to bring it back from the verge of bankruptcy...yet she had no one to share all the triumphs and tribulations with.

She didn't have the man she loved. And Daniel didn't have the man who was his true father. A dad who would love him and guide him with a gentle but firm hand. Didn't she owe Daniel that much? Didn't she deserve to be happy with the man she loved? The only man she'd ever loved.

"Oh, Tyler," she whispered miserably. "What have we done?" Were they both so full of pride and hurt that nothing would breach the chasm of old, painful memories between them?

As if her thoughts conjured him, Brianne watched his truck and trailer drive down the dirt road to the stables. Her heart pounded so hard in her chest it hurt, and she had to refrain from the urge to run outside and throw herself into his arms and never let go.

Had he decided to return for Roman Warrior after all?

He got out of the truck, and before he'd taken five steps Daniel was out of the corral and racing toward him. Her son catapulted himself against his chest, and Tyler hugged him fiercely.

A huge lump formed in her chest. The love between the two of them was obvious and very painful to watch. Is this what she had to endure every time Tyler decided to visit? If so, it was going to kill her.

Tyler said something to Daniel and her son pointed toward the office. With an affectionate tug on Daniel's Stetson, a few more words, and a wave toward Jasper, Tyler headed in her direction, his stride purposeful. It was then she noticed the piece of paper in his hand and wondered if this was, indeed, purely a business meeting.

He entered the office and closed the door behind him, then turned and met her gaze. "Hello, Bree."

There was no animosity in his dark blue eyes, unlike the day he'd left. Instead, she detected a possessiveness that unnerved her and made her immediately defensive.

"Tyler," she acknowledged, moving away from the window and back behind the safety of her desk. She had no right to ask him what he was doing here, considering he still owned half the ranch. "Just in the neighborhood?'' she said, striving for a lightness she was far from feeling.

"You could say that," he said, slowly moving toward her. "I was paying a visit to our lawyer and I thought I'd drop this off." Standing across from her, he let the piece of paper in his hand drift to the surface of her desk. "What do you think?"

Curious, she picked up the legal-looking document, and when she realized what it was, her hand began to tremble. Through a haze of oncoming tears, she stared at the deed granting Daniel Tyler's share of Whitmore Acres.

"What's this for?" she asked in a strained voice, though the significance of the document was achingly clear. Tyler was presenting her with the opportunity to sever all ties to him.

"It's what you wanted," he said steadily, his gaze giving away nothing. "Complete independence and stability."

Her breath caught at his selfless gift, when she'd done nothing but think of herself and allow her fears to overrule her heart. Tyler was willing to give up his dreams for her!

"No," she said, shaking her head. "I can't let you do this."

"No?" He lifted a brow, but he seemed surprisingly stoic for a man who was giving up his home. "It's a done deal, Bree. Signed, sealed, and delivered."

She wanted to ask him if this was it, the last time either she or Daniel would see him, but she couldn't get the words past the tightness in her throat.

"Oh, I almost forgot," he said, frowning as he pushed his Stetson back on his head. "The deed comes with a stipulation."

She frowned and glanced back at the document, looking for a fine print and finding none. "What kind of stipulation?"

Crossing his arms over his chest, he swept his gaze over her. "That I get you and Daniel in return."

She sucked in a startled breath, certain she'd misheard him. "What are you talking about, Tyler?"

"I'm talking about being a family. I won't settle for less." He started around her desk, his steps as determined as the light in his eyes. "I never should have left."

"I pushed you away," she admitted, anticipation filling her as he neared. "I was so afraid you'd never forgive me, for marrying Boyd, and raising Daniel as his son."

"Ah, Brianne." Reaching her, he gathered her in his arms and held her so close she could feel the fast beating of his heart. "So much hurt."

She closed her eyes and absorbed his warmth and tenderness. "I should have trusted you with the truth."

"Yes, you should have," he said, a smile in his voice.

She pulled back slightly, awed by the deep devotion shining in his eyes. "Can you ever forgive me?"

His fingers touched her cheek in a reverent caress. "I already have."

Relief flooded her. Moving from his embrace, she tore the deed into four squares and stuffed the scraps of paper into the front pocket of his jeans.

"You don't want the ranch?" he asked.

"What good is the ranch, and everything else when I don't have the man I love? You're all I'll ever want. I do trust you, Tyler," she whispered, knowing it was true. "And I love you."

He smiled as though she'd given him a rare treasure. "That's all I needed to hear, and that's all we need to make it together."

"You think so?" she asked, reflecting on all the hurt and anger they'd endured over the years.

He framed her face in his hands, his gaze dark, intense and brimming with love. "The past is the past. We've both made mistakes. Now, let's make memories."

Her heart was so full, it crowded her chest. "Wonderful memories," she amended.

A sinful grin curved his mouth. "Yeah," he agreed, just as his mouth covered hers in a hot, deep kiss that burned any lingering doubts she might have had into cinders.

When he finally let her up for air, she pressed her forehead against his, gulping for breath. She glided her hands up his muscular arms, touching him, wanting to make up for all the days without him. "I'm sorry for being so stubborn and blind."

He brushed a soft kiss across her lips, then lifted his head. "You're scared, and I know that. We're gonna have our share of arguments, but you have to know I would never intentionally hurt you."

"I know that." As reluctant as she was to leave his arms, there was still one last issue to settle. She held out her hand to him. "I think it's time Daniel met his real father."

"Yeah," he said, and slipped his hand securely in hers.

Together they went back outside and found Daniel by Tyler's trailer with Jasper.

"You brought Sweet Justice," Daniel said, hope filling his voice. "Are you staying, Uncle Tyler?"

Tyler glanced at Brianne, leaving the momentous task of answering that question up to her.

"Yes, he's staying," she said, a case of full-blown nerves making her voice quiver. "But there's something I need to tell you, Daniel."

He glanced from Tyler to his mother. "What is it, Mom?"

The moment of truth had come, and it felt amazingly right. "Daniel..." she said, beginning the introduction that would change the course of his entire life. For the better. "This is your father, Tyler Whitmore."

"Uncle Tyler is my dad?" Disbelief shifted across his features. "Really?"

"Yes, really," she whispered.

Tyler took a step toward Daniel, then hesitated. "My son," he said, his voice shaky with emotion.

Tyler's words were all the prompting Daniel needed. "Dad!" he said, sprinting the short distance into Tyler's arms, openly welcoming him with his affectionate display.

"Well, it's about damn time," Jasper muttered.

The incredible joy enveloping Tyler's expression brought tears to Brianne's eyes. And then she laughed, because the moment seemed so perfect. Questions and explanations would come later, she knew, but for now, she was satisfied with the happy reunion.

After a long, emotion-filled moment, son and father broke apart. Tyler straightened and settled his gaze on Brianne. "If I'm going to be Daniel's dad, what do you say we make it legal?"

Brianne held her breath, wondering if her dreams of nine years ago would finally come true, that she'd be Tyler's wife and grow old with him. "Is that a proposal?"

He came to her. "Yes," he said, gently pushing a strand of hair behind her ear. "You're my life. My love. Will you marry me, Brianne?"

"Yes," she replied as an indescribable happiness cas-

caded over her. She smiled, thinking how far they'd
come and how bright the future looked. "Oh, yes. I love
you, Tyler Whitmore," she whispered.

Tyler had returned. This time for good.

EPILOGUE

"AND the winner of the Junior Cheney Reining Championship is Daniel Whitmore, riding Sweet Justice," the announcer said over the loudspeakers posted in the huge outdoor arena. The audience applauded and cheered the nine-year-old boy who'd showed superb reining skills.

Tyler surged to his feet, letting out a whoop and a holler that had Brianne laughing, and people staring. A huge grin encompassed his face, and pride shone in his eyes as he watched Daniel accept his trophy. Daniel turned on the platform, gleaming trophy in one hand, and gave his dad a thumbs-up sign.

"Way to go, son!" Tyler hollered, then gave a shrill whistle.

Tears of happiness gathered in Brianne's eyes. She and Tyler had been married for a little less than a year, and each day that passed she loved him more. She couldn't imagine life without him, and knew she never would. Tyler was in this family for the long haul.

"That's my boy," Tyler said to the spectators around them. He grabbed the box of cigars he'd insisted on buying on the way to the competition, telling Brianne he'd need them when his son took the purse. Grinning like a fool, he handed a cigar to the man beside him. "That's my boy," he said again.

A grin quirked the older man's face. "He's a mighty fine rider," he said.

"Yeah, I know," Tyler said proudly. "He takes after his dad."

Brianne sat on the wooden bench as Tyler continued handing out the cigars until they were gone, all the while boasting about Daniel's riding skills. The afternoon was warm, making the queasiness plaguing Brianne for the past couple of days more pronounced.

Once the excitement settled, Tyler turned to Brianne, his exhilarated expression turning to a frown. "Are you okay, Bree? You look pale."

"I'm fine. Too much sun, I think." She gave him a smile, wondering how and when to tell him her news. They'd decided to wait another year before having a baby, until the reining operation was completely solvent and they had a decent savings to fall back on. Actually, it had been her suggestion, but Tyler hadn't argued, knowing her worries for security. Now, she realized she wasn't sure what Tyler's reaction would be to having a baby.

"Let's go get you something to drink," he suggested. "How 'bout a cool glass of lemonade?"

"Sounds good." Brianne stood, and Tyler tucked her hand in the crook of his arm as they headed toward the concession stand. On the way they stopped at a vendor's booth where Tyler bought Daniel his first pair of leather chaps.

"You're spoiling him," Brianne admonished gently as they started on their way again.

"It's my duty as his dad to spoil him," he replied unapologetically as his fingers caressed the hand in his arm, then traced the gold wedding band on her finger.

"I hope you won't mind having one more to spoil," she said in a casual tone.

Tyler stopped abruptly, his gaze searching her face. A spark of hope glimmered in his eyes. "What are you talking about?"

She took a deep breath, unsure if the butterflies in her

stomach were due to nerves, or her condition. "I'm pregnant."

Tyler stared at Brianne, stunned at her announcement. He pulled her to the side, out of the way of the crowd of people in the concession area. "But we've always been careful," he said in a low voice.

A blush stole over her cheeks. "Not the time in the barn."

Remembering the wild, impetuous lovemaking of that evening nearly two months ago, and his wife's wanton behavior as she'd unexpectedly seduced him while he'd been attending Roman Warrior, he grinned. "No, we didn't, did we?"

She shook her head sheepishly, then bit her lip, suddenly looking uncertain. "I know this wasn't planned. Do you mind?"

"Do I mind?" he asked incredulously. "Oh, baby, the only thing I mind is not getting you pregnant sooner. Are you ready for this?"

She touched her fingertips to his jaw, love shining in her eyes. "As long as we're in it together."

"Always," he said, knowing that would be a vow he kept until the end of forever. "A baby," he said in awe, tentatively pressing his large hand to her still-flat stomach encased in jeans.

"Our baby," she whispered.

A fierce pride, like nothing he'd ever known, surged through him. "She's pregnant," he announced to the public, then louder, "My wife is pregnant!"

The crowd witnessing Tyler's declaration cheered and issued congratulations. Brianne laughed and wrapped her arms around him, sighing contentedly into his ear. "I love you, Tyler Whitmore," she said.

"And I love you." He kissed her, a slow, sweet kiss for the world to see. "Ah, Bree," he murmured against her lips, basking in the strength of their love. "Life doesn't get any better than this."

Seven and a half months later, holding his baby girl in his arms, Tyler realized life did, indeed, get richer with every passing day.

Question: How do you find the sexy cowboy of your dreams?

Answer: Read on....

Texas Grooms Wanted!
is a brand-new miniseries from

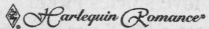 *Harlequin Romance*

Meet three very special heroines who are all looking for very special Texas men—their future husbands! Good men may be hard to find, but these women have experts on hand. They've all signed up with the Yellow Rose Matchmakers. The oldest and the best matchmaking service in San Antonio, Texas, the Yellow Rose guarantees to find any woman her perfect partner....

So for the cutest cowboys in the whole state of Texas, look out for:

HAND-PICKED HUSBAND
by Heather MacAllister in January 1999

BACHELOR AVAILABLE!
by Ruth Jean Dale in February 1999

THE NINE-DOLLAR DADDY
by Day Leclaire in March 1999

Only cowboys need apply...

Available wherever
Harlequin Romance books
are sold.

If you enjoyed what you just read,
then we've got an offer you can't resist!

Take 2 bestselling love stories FREE!

Plus get a FREE surprise gift!

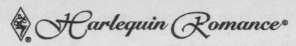

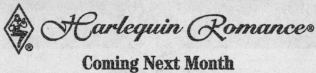

Coming Next Month

#3547 DADDY AND DAUGHTERS Barbara McMahon
Jared Hunter had just discovered he had not one but *two* adorable two-year-old daughters he'd known nothing about! Cassie Bowles was more than willing to help this bachelor dad with his newfound family. But could she accept his marriage proposal, knowing he only wanted a mother for his daughters?

Daddy Boom: *Who says bachelors and babies don't mix?*

#3548 BEAUTY AND THE BOSS Lucy Gordon
Parted temporarily from those he relied on—his young daughter, Alison, and his beloved guide dog—Craig Locksley was forced to accept Delia's offer of help. So Delia found herself living with an impossibly grumpy but incredibly attractive man. She wanted to love him—if only he'd let her....

Marrying the Boss: *From boardroom...to bride and groom!*

Introducing the second part of Rebecca Winters's wonderful new trilogy:

#3549 UNDERCOVER BACHELOR Rebecca Winters
Gerard Roch had given up on love since the death of his first wife. Going undercover to catch a thief, he never expected to find himself attracted to an eighteen-year-old temptress. But was Whitney Lawrence really what she seemed...?

Love Undercover: *Their mission was marriage!*

#3550 HER OWN PRINCE CHARMING Eva Rutland
Brad Vandercamp is a millionaire English playboy so glamorous that his nickname is Prince! And when Paula meets him at a glittering masked ball, she realizes that she could have found her very own Prince Charming. But they are worlds apart—she's poor, he's rich. Could he really want her for his bride?